Just a Thought Away

A Novel

Dianne Zimmermann

Publishing Assistance
BookCrafters, Parker, Colorado.
www.BookCrafters.net

*I dedicate this book to my friends
whose never-ending encouragement
drove me on when the going got tough.*

Acknowledgements

I wish to thank my friends for all their interest and encouragement in all my writing endeavors. Just a Thought Away is my sixth book. I wish to express special thanks to my friends Lou Platten and LA Mott for their years of encouragement, ideas, proofreading, and editing skills.

Chapter One

What happened? Margo remembered driving down the county road heading into town to go to the grocery store for Jack. She was rushing to the grocery store because her husband insisted on spaghetti and Italian sausage, complete with side-salad fixings for dinner. Of course, she had none of those ingredients at home. She wished he would have wanted something else for dinner that she already had the ingredients for, like chicken vegetable soup or pork sausage, mashed potatoes, and sauerkraut. She was not looking forward to driving since it was raining. Jack was in a bad mood again, so to appease him, she quickly made a list, jumped in the car, and headed into town in the pouring rain. And now suddenly out of nowhere, she lay in shock, struggling to breath.

Margo laid trapped in her overturned partially submerged vehicle in murky water up to her neck. She was cold, wet and scared. *What just happened?* It all happened so fast. One moment she was driving in the rain down the rain slick county road and the next moment she is lying practically upside down in the submerged overturned car. Her head hurt where she thought she must have hit it on the steering wheel at one point as the car tumbled end over end down the embankment into the murky water. *Am I going to die?* Margo was choking as water was rising and getting into her mouth. She prayed as she felt she was about to pass out.

She felt lightheaded as if she was rising into space. *Was she dying? Did she die?* She looked down and saw her body in the car below her submerged in the flood waters. Rising up she felt a sharp spark of energy.

She saw the light above, drawing her up. As her body rose up into the night toward the stars, she felt light, almost weightless. She drifted up into the ethereal, drawn by the bright light. To her surprise, she was greeted by loving soul spirits. Her heart swelled with love as their lovely faces glowed with bright smiles. She felt their loving embrace. She felt at home and loved it there in the warm bright light surrounded by loved ones.

"It's so beautiful here," Margo was astonished by the all-encompassing heavenly glowing feelings of love that surrounded her.

"You must go back," urged a soft feminine voice in the light, "as you have much work to do for the people of your generation and beyond."

"Why, must I go back? I wish to stay here," cried Margo wanting to stay surrounded in the warmth of the loving light.

"Margo, it is not your time yet, your work on Earth is

not yet finished" the soft voice of her collective guides and past loved ones told her.

Margo was having a near-death experience. It wasn't her time to leave the Earth. She didn't quit understand it, but Margo was a volunteer hybrid, a Pleiadian hybrid, from the Pleiades star system. She was a Pleiadian spirit born on earth to experience being a human being. She and others like her were needed on planet Earth to help calm the overpowering negative bright white masculine Reptilian Anunnaki energy that permeated throughout the world. The Anunnaki ruled Fourth Dimension was made up of the negative energy of corporate greed, racial prejudice, and social discontent. Religious and political arenas were filled with negativity.

Enslaved minorities, including women, on Earth, were experiencing the ending of the Fourth Dimension patriarchal authoritarian rule. This is the ascendants of the Reptilian Anunnaki rule last-ditch effort to dominate humans, and they are failing. Anunnaki Reptilian creatures of the patriarchal rule Fourth Dimension are dying out but making one last-ditch effort to dominate the world by restricting wages, education and using other methods to dumb down the population and make them docile and easy to manipulate in their efforts to bring about global rule.

"What?" Margo asked. She was in a daze but could still marvel at her heavenly surroundings of love and light.

"This is the dawning of the feminine rule of the age

of Aquarius, the Fifth Dimension. We will help you," the heavenly voice in the bright light said.

"But, what can I do?" Margo said slowly as she felt herself drifting back into her injured body.

In a flash Margo felt that she was back in the submerged car reunited with her body. She regained consciousness and began to gasp for breath. She knew it was a near-death experience in which she left her body for a few moments; she knew it because she had had one once before when Jack beat her so severely that she was in intensive care in the hospital for days. She was a survivor then, and she would survive this now too.

She choked as the water rose up around her inside her car, and her footing slipped and her mouth and nose went under. She struggled to move up and better position herself. She laid on her back in a twisted fashion as she was caught in her seat belt, which somehow had tightened around her neck making it difficult for her to move. She had a weird primal sensation, as if she were floating in embryonic fluid in a womb with the umbilical cord wrapped around her neck. She knew she had to think of something and fast, as she laid in a constrained and awkwardly twisted position. She was submerged in bone chilling silent murkiness and she could feel the water rising higher ever so slowly around her neck. She tried not to panic.

She felt weak and faint and wanted to pass out but the cold water like a slap in the face brought her back to full consciousness. She smelled motor oil and gasoline mixed with the water and that scared her. She knew she had to get out right away as the water was rising inside the overturned partially submerged vehicle. Quickly, she made efforts to adjust her mental orientation to coincide with her twisted upside-down position. Feeling all around as much as she could, she tried to find the release button for the seat belt. Struggle as she may, she could not get close enough to the back corner of the seat to find it. She was getting more and more concerned as the water was rising higher and higher. Margo gave up and felt around for the console release button located between the driver's seat and the passenger seat. She knew she had a very special tool in the console. It could very well save her life. It was a tool that she had bought by chance one day while visiting an auto supply store looking for window cleaner and car wax.

The tool was double ended. One end of the tool was a window breaking hammer and on the other end of the tool was a sharp razor that could slice through tough seat belt material. Was it some sort of a premonition that she had recently purchased the tool on a whim? Was it intuition? Did her subconscious know this day was coming? Was the guy shopping next to her in the auto supply store that day a guardian angel, or her spirit guide.

The man had smiled and said hello and struck up a conversation with her about which car wax and window cleaner he liked best. He thought he would help as he seen that she was trying to decide which one to buy. As they chatted, she noticed that he was looking at the seat belt and window smashing tool and she too began to wonder if it might be a good idea to get one to keep in her car.

"What is that you are looking at?" she had asked him out of curiosity. "It looks rather interesting."

"It's a seat belt cutter and a window smashing tool," he replied turning it over in his hand to give her a better look at it.

"Oh, in case you are trapped in your seat belt in your car and can't get out," she said when she realized what it was to be used for.

"Yes, and the other end is used to shatter window glass," he added.

"It sure looks like a pretty handy gadget to have," Margo replied.

"Yes, it does. Well you never know, we certainly have been getting lots of rain lately, and with all this flooding happening around here, it can't be a bad idea," the kind stranger said. His face turned rather serious as did hers when they heard a sudden loud clap of thunder lead way to the deafening sound of heavy rain hitting the metal roof of the store.

"It just might be a good idea." The man repeated shouting against the thunderous racket on the metal roof. They looked at each other and rolled their eyes as they watched the heavy rain drench the parking lot.

"Certainly can't hurt to have one in the car," Margo said with a smile.

"That does it, I am getting one of these," the man said.

"Me too." She took one of the tools off the hanging

rack to buy for herself. Dashing to her car when there was a break in the down pour, she put the tool in the console between the front seats. And now as she struggled in the submerged vehicle, she wondered, had he been a guardian angel, sent by her spirit guides? The thought gave her hope that she might survive somehow even as she practically hung upside down trapped in rising flood water. She thanked the universe for that guardian angel who pointed out that tool to her.

It had been a very unusual rainy spring season and the television news had reported drivers not adhering to warnings and driving through flooded areas and that could be very dangerous. *No kidding,* she thought. She thought back on that moment in that store when that man suggested it was a good idea to have the seat belt cutter and glass breaking tool in the car. She was so glad she bought one, now to try to get it out of the console where she had put it.

She thought she could use a little more extra help and she prayed. She could not reach the seat belt release button, so she tried to maneuver over closer to the console. She asked her guides to help her. She wiggled around keeping her head above the slowly rising water that was filling the car. She just had to maneuver closer somehow so she could reach the console. First she had to figure out her orientation in the turned over upside-down nearly totally submerged car.

Margo could see out the bottom of back window that was still above water. She could easily spot the full moon through a break in the storm clouds. It was a blue moon, as it was the second full moon in the same month. It made her think of the saying, "once in a blue moon" and the song titled "Blue Moon" which she began to hum in her head.

Yeah, once in a blue moon do you get forced off the road, in the rain, in the dark into flooded waters. *So much for global warming,* she thought. All her life she had lived in this area and had never seen torrential downpours like they had seen lately. The rain had suddenly stopped and clouds separated. The moon shown brightly and reflected on the flooded water that surrounded her. The moon was such a heavenly, friendly sight that somehow gave her a little more hope even as the water slowly but steadily rose around her.

But, her hope was fleeing fast, as she was becoming more frightened by each fraction of an inch of water that continued to rise. The space around her was an air pocket and she thanked the heavens for it, her spiritual guides, and the Pleiadians that she believed in. The comforting glow of the full moon breaking through the clouds comforted her a bit now, just when she needed it most. It gave her hope and she knew that somehow she was going to make it out of the submerged vehicle to safety. She considered the man in the auto supply store a spiritual guide for he pointed out the seat belt cutting tool. Little did she realize at the time that the seat belt cutting and glass chattering tool would one day help save her life. She knew her spiritual guides had helped her then and would help her now. She had always believed in spirit guides, archangels and extraterrestrials and knew that the Pleiadians, the silent protectors of planet Earth, from the Pleiades star cluster in the Taurus constellation, were with her now too.

Through the years, she had loved learning about the Fourth Dimension evil Anunnaki Reptilian races cast down from Mars to be slaveholders of a sort on planet Earth. They were everywhere in dictatorship governments and behind the scenes shaping an anti-democracy mindset in America and in other countries around the world. Each fascism dictatorship that is established will one day fight to conquer the other, resulting into a one world dictatorship.

But, where there was bad there was promising good coming with the dawning of the Fifth Dimension which would be feminine ruled by the Pleiadians. The Pleiadians are soul healers and protectors of planet Earth. If things should get too dire and they fear the possible destruction of the planet, they will respond in order to save it. There was a time during a threat of war that they came and encircled several missile warheads and with laser light disarmed them. It all was caught on video which was hidden away for years. Through the years commercial airline pilots have spotted unidentifiable foreign objects, they called UFOs. The pilots knew their reporting of UFO's would be denied, so for fear of losing their jobs and their pilot licenses, they never reported the UFOs to officials. UFOs come from all over the galaxy. The Pleiadians are one of the good guides that come to rescue planet Earth.

Hopefully they save it in time before the narcissistic, egotistical Anunnaki Reptilian human hybrids can completely ruin it out of sheer ignorance, greed, and carelessness.

Margo agreed that according to UFO websites, women are more open to the thought of aliens and UFO sightings, as they choose to believe aliens as more benevolent rather than a threat. She noticed that most women think that if the far more advanced aliens from other planets can get to Earth, and if they were a threat to humankind, we would have been dead by now. On the other hand, men, according to Margo's observations through the years, seemed to be more reactive feeling threatened by UFO's and aliens and want to destroy them. It had appeared to Margo that some men, like her husband, were just pure geniuses, never wrong, always right, nothing was ever their fault and always blamed others, and want to kill what they don't understand. To Margo, that was just plain primitive Reptilian Anunnaki defense behavior that continues even to this day; she was appalled.

Margo couldn't believe that human beings were still hostile and had not evolved much at all over decades and centuries. It's the twenty-first century, and human beings are still fighting and killing each other. Of course Margo saw all things through her own eyes, as everyone does. Seeing things personally through her own experience, Margo thought it was the same with men in marriages. It's like women were property, she thought in much dismay. Her husband Jack had to constantly know her every move and whereabouts. He subtly verbally abused her over and over again gradually breaking her spirit. It was his subconscious effort to make sure she did not have confidence enough to ever leave him. So, in Margo's experience, she found that Jack pretty much did what he wanted, and she just went along with his ideas. It was just easier for her to follow the path of least resistance.

Margo was depressed and wanted to get off the planet. Earth was just too hard; as it was made up of too many barbaric males she thought, too much war, hate and greed. Margo wondered why men were as they were. Of course there were the good guys; just like there are bad women. But no one group stood out as wrong doers in Margo's mind as privileged white males.

Margo was curious and did a lot of research as to why the male population were as they seemed, angry and seemed to be in fear of losing their pure white godlike self-proclaimed superiority. What she learned was that in ancient times Mars was hit by a Reptilian comet attack that stripped off most of the Martian atmosphere threatening the existence of life on Mars. Tired of living underground and having spacefaring technology, Martians merely found a new home on planet Earth. So they all migrated to Earth and colonized a place called Sumer. There is a galactic federation which had a population of Lyra expatriates on Earth to suppress the Reptilians that were there. The Sumerians aka 4600 BCE left behind clay tablet text that later were carefully deciphered, and much was learned.

Martians interbred with the Anunnaki and Reptilian hybrid humans on Earth which diluted the DNA. The humans of Sumer viewed the Martians as gods, so their off-spring were considered mighty males thus we have those Martian types remaining here on Earth now, in modern times. The Sumerians knew about the flood that destroyed Atlantis according to the clay tablets. The galactic federation settled the Martians on Earth to maintain a human hybrid presence there to contain the Reptilians after the destruction of Atlantis. The Martians protected the human population from the resurgence of the Reptilians emerging from their underground shelters. The Anunnaki were also of Reptilian origin and were influencing the human species. The Anunnaki Reptilians were planning their takeover of the surface world through war and greed working to create a New World Order oligarchy during the Fourth Dimension of the Pisces Reptilian Anunnaki rule. This was established to polarize humans on Earth and have them fighting amongst themselves. Thus we have the conditions on Earth that we have today: greed, war, racism, and misogyny. And that is what makes up the patriarchal rule of the fourth dimension. But a new dawn has broken, the dawning of the Age of Aquarius. Now we are in the Fifth Dimension of Pleiadians feminine rule and the Age of Aquarius. An age where men and women will become more androgynous in looks and behavior, and more equal in their social status.

Chapter Two

Margo recalled reading that the Pleiadians had a substation on the dark side of the moon, and she believed it because she felt connected as she thought of their energy whenever she looked up at the moon. She looked at the moon now through the dirty, partially shattered rear window and hoped that they knew she was in trouble and about to drown in an overturned car and would come to help her somehow.

What the hell, Margo thought in desperation. She worried for her survival as she made one last attempt to locate the seat belt release button, which appeared to be just out of reach of her finger tips. *But right next to the seat belt release button was the console and its lid release button was closer to her,* she thought. She decided to give up on trying to find the seat belt release button. She thought, maybe, just maybe she could reach and push the button to unlatch the console lid. The console positioned between the two front seats was just in her reach.

With the seat belt stretched tight around her neck, she could barely move much less reach far enough to touch the console, but she persevered and stretched the seat belt as far as she could. She felt around in the murky water for the console lid release. She poked around everywhere because she did not know exactly where the latch was located. After poking with her finger every possible inch of the console lip, she finally hit the release button. Ever so slowly the lid sprung open pushing against the pressure of the rising water. Her things began to move and drift out of the console. Cash, candy, pills, lots of coins, began slowly drifting out of the console into the water around her. Wet five and ten dollar bills floated about and drifted off into the dark car and murky water. She was too distracted to care about trying to retrieve any of the money. Instead, she looked around for the seatbelt cutting tool. Suddenly it fell out of the console toward her. She jumped when it bumped her hand but managed to grab on to it tightly, never minding the sharp razor edge that she knew was on the tool somewhere. She got the tool in her hand just in time as it was she thought, she was beginning to feel panicky.

The water level was rising higher and higher around her neck. The pocket of air above her head was becoming smaller and further out of reach. It was getting so high now that she had to bob and kick to rise up far enough to take in a deep breath of air. She kicked herself up and quickly took several deep breaths. She hoped that the air pocket above her would remain reachable for a few more minutes. She knew she had to work fast.

The precious tool that she now held tightly in her hand would hopefully save her life. She felt for the razor edge of the tool and found it opposite the pointed end used to break the glass. She reached around in the cold murky water and grabbed the seat belt strap with her left hand and with her right fiercely began making sawing motions. She could not see what she was doing so she was just trying not to slip and cut herself. Her prayers to the Pleiadians and her spiritual guides were as constant and fierce as were her sawing motions.

Margo was spiritual and faulted religion for all the inhuman idealisms she had to unlearn. She no longer participated in what she thought were manipulating and controlling patriarchal, authoritarian, racist, and misogynistic white privileged religious ways. Instead, she preferred learning about all things metaphysical and extraterrestrial.

Margo believed in the seven sisters Pleiades star cluster. Subaru is the Japanese name for the Pleiades star cluster M45, or the "Seven Sisters" one of which is not visible since only six of the stars are visible. Six of the seven stars are featured on the Subaru emblem, including the brightest central star called Alcyone. Somehow the Pleiades star system resonated with Margo the moment she read about it. For some reason, when Margo discovered the Pleiades constellation, she felt connected and the sense of familiarity. Actually, unbeknownst to Margo till later, she was originally from the Pleiades before she birthed on Earth as a Pleiadian human hybrid.

Margo continued to pray as she vigorously sawed through the tough seat belt material. It was working, she could feel the material fray as it began to split away. She was making progress, but she knew that she had to work fast as she felt the eerie feeling of rising water. The seat belt still stretched against her neck. She was thankful for the moonlight although dim and fuzzy seen through the dirty cracked rear window of the car. She struggled with panic and fear, as the murky water was up to her ears. Desperately she tried to peer through its murkiness to see what her hands were touching but gave up trying to see what she was doing and worked mostly by feel. She feverishly made sawing motions. Finally, she felt the cloth give way and split and felt the fraying ends against her fingers.

Finally! She thought she couldn't hold her breath one more second, when she felt the belt give way and break loose. She felt miraculously freed and it gave her hope. In one quick motion she rose up and gasped for air taking in a huge deep breath. She cried and prayed to the universe to help her. She held tightly onto the tool that set her free and saved her life. It was her lifeline to survival and she thanked the man who appeared in the auto supply store and brought her attention to buying the life-saving glass shattering and seat belt cutting tool.

Margo took several more deep breaths to calm herself down as she saw the rising water allowing the air space in her car become smaller and smaller. She was startled and jumped when the car shifted a bit with the slow but forceful current. For a moment she feared the car would break free and drift off with her in it. Anxiously she looked around in the car for an escape route. The earlier angry-looking storm clouds had broken up and now the moon appeared brightly illuminating the confines of her potential aquatic grave. The car shifted again in the rising swift current. It was clear to Margo, that she needed to escape this death trap and fast.

She thought about crawling closer and smashing out the partially submerged back window to get out but changed her mind when she thought of the large volume of water that would rush in on her and maybe dislodge the car, and she would float away in it. Instead, she decided to make use of the small pocket of air, that still existed but was fast becoming smaller. She hurried and took another deep breath from the air pocket. She thanked her guides along with the moon sighting that brought her a bit of comfort in her dreadful situation. She thought the front side window frame was large enough for her to slide through. It took her a moment as she lost her bearings to figure out which side of the car was closest to the embankment, as the car had tumbled end over end and rested on its roof. She decided that driver's side window was her best choice. She hoped that her gambled estimation was correct and that the driver's side of the car was closest to the embankment. She hoped and prayed with all her strength. And with all the strength and muster she could gather while in water up to her ears, she raised her arm as high as she could aiming the pointed glass breaking end of the tool and brought her arm down as hard as she could. It worked!

To her amazement one good hard whack at it worked, and the window shattered to pieces and drifted out into the murky water flowing by. Margo was so excited that it worked and gave her an escape route.

She reached about in the water and found her small shoulder strapped handbag she had slipped around the steering wheel for safe keeping. She quickly slipped her arm through the strap then over her head and across her chest to make sure it wouldn't drift away. Quickly she moved, and easily pushed her head and body out through the open window as water rushed in all around her. She paddled her arms and kicked her legs and feet forcing her in an upward direction. To her delight, she knew she would make it now. She was free. She felt aided and guided by a magical spiritual force as she escaped the confines of her watery graveyard.

Margo felt the presence of the Pleiadians along with her spiritual guides helping her to find her way in the dim light of the moon. She felt as if she had help. It was as if the current pulled her out and up. In a second, her head was out of the water. She took in deep breaths of air as if it was the most precious commodity she could ever behold. The clouds were separating and the moon presented itself lighting up the night. She looked around as well as she could. There was water everywhere. Flood waters created lakes where there once were none. The soybean and corn fields she had driven past every day to go to her job at the real estate office were gone, and there was water everywhere. The whole lower area looked like one big lake as it reflected the moonlight. The recent weeks' record breaking heavy rains strained the capacity of the roadside ditches.

The crops were ruined. Sadly there would be no profits to be made for farmers this year, and farmers' mounting bills would have to wait payment. She was filled with sorrow and dread for the farmers loss of revenue. She had remembered seeing the fields look so plush and thick promising bumper crops yields. But then the heavy torrential rain moved in.

Margo splashed about half trying to swim, half trying to walk, kicking her feet to find the ground so she could get her footing. To her amazement, she somehow worked her way over to the embankment where she struggled to get better footing in the soft mud. With determination, she managed to hang on to the tall weeds and pulled and crawled her way up and out of the muddy water onto the embankment. She felt weak and tired but somehow managed to grab and hold onto small tree limbs and saplings as she slipped and pawed her way up the steep muddy hillside. The night was cold, and her wet body shivered as she pulled herself up out of the water.

She was cold and weighted down by soaking wet, muddy clothes. She felt bruised and scratched, but she nevertheless persisted and clawed her way up. Finally after struggling for what seems like hours, she made it to the roadway. She collapsed and laid on her side catching her breath and breathing heavily from exhaustion. She laid there feeling numb and other worldly all alone in the night. She laid there listening to her own breath and the sounds of the night. The rain had stopped but water was dripping from the trees onto the roadway. Rhythmic sounds of tree frogs, crickets and cicadas sounds filled the night air. The sounds were soothing to her as was the sight of the full moon peeking through a break in the clouds overhead.

Margo was grateful for the moon glow as she raised her head and looked all around. There were no headlights or taillights in sight in either direction. In a way she was glad because if some driver would have come along with a rifle in his truck, he probably would have taken a shot at her thinking she was a potential roadkill or an aquatic monster that had crawled out of the darkened lagoon. As she laid there covered with mud, moss, and leaves hanging from her hair, she felt all alone, frightened, but was grateful to be alive. She cried as she thanked her lucky stars, the angels, her spirit guides, the Pleiadians and everyone else she could think of. Margo always thought of herself as a spiritual person rather than a religious person. She favored alternative beliefs after having read many books about life after death, reincarnation and near-death experiences.

Margo laid alongside the road wishing a car would come by with a kind driver to help her. As she waited, she wondered about her husband Jack. Would he wonder where she was and come looking for her. Did he think to go ahead and fix himself something to eat. Would he be sorry that he sent her out into the rainy night to go to the grocery store, because he wanted to eat something special that they did not have at home?

Would he be out looking for her? She doubted it. As of late they were not getting along and he spent more and more time away from home. Several months after they were married, he became angry and argumentative. And as time went on, he became violent at times. He began hitting her. The beatings got worse, until one day, he beat her into a coma. She'd be dead if the neighbors had not heard the commotion and called the police. At the time the police said she should have pressed charges and have her husband arrested. She didn't because she was afraid to. The nurses who took care of her told her she should leave him. But he had cried and apologized profusely. So she forgave him, again. Margo's husband Jack gave her such low self-esteem, always mocking her, making fun of her that at times she just felt like a mindless walking zombie around him. No matter what she tried to do to please him, he always got angry. It was all her fault for aggravating him. And each time it got more violent. Because the longer she put up with him the more he hated her for it and wanted to punch her harder for tolerating his bad behavior.

Jack had beaten her while he was in a drunken fit of anger. He could have easily killed her. Margo's injuries were so severe that she ended up in surgery for hours and a hospital stay for days. As doctors struggled to save her, Margo had a near-death experience while she was under anesthesia. Her heart stopped and she left her body and rose up to the ceiling. She floated upward above the operating table and watched the surgeons operate to remove a blood clot. Later while speaking with medical personnel, she described the doctors and nurses and the procedures they performed while she was unconscious. Margo was a different person now, she no longer feared death. Doctors had known about near-death experiences for years having heard similar details from many other patients. At the time the hospital psychologist told her that from what she described, she indeed had a near-,death experience. She had seen the bright light tunnel taking her up to where she saw her deceased loved ones. It was beautiful and loving there and she did not want to leave. But a voice told her she had to go back, that it was not her time yet and that she still had things to do. It was painful to come back into her tired and battered body. But from that day on, Margo was not afraid to die. She became more curious than anything about what happens to a soul when the body dies. Laying there now alongside the road she had time to think about past experiences and wonder why these things had happened to her.

Margo thought back to how she was forced off the road. She was just driving into town to get a few groceries for dinner, because Jack wanted spaghetti with Italian sausage, when the accident happened. The driver who hit her drove on. So she figured that no one knew that she was out there all alone laying on the wet pavement. No one knew that she had been forced off the road and down an embankment. And that her car laid upside down and submerged in the deep dark cold murky water.

She blinked back tears recalling how she was driving

along slower than the speed limit because of the dark and rainy conditions. She was being careful and minding her own business, when she was viciously sideswiped by a big pickup truck. The truck came up fast behind her. The driver tailgated her for a bit, then swiftly and recklessly swerved around her. Margo thought the driver appeared to misjudge the space between their two vehicles, and in an attempt to move back into the right lane cut back over too soon and clipped the front driver side of her car and knocked her car out of control. She remembered that she had been afraid something might happen as she had seen him coming up fast behind her. The truck sat higher than her car and its blinding bright headlights shined in her rearview mirror and her outside driver side mirror so bright that she was practically unable to see where she was driving.

Her stomach tightened in terror, as she wondered why someone was driving so fast and reckless on such a rainy night. She remembered that when the truck began to come around, she thought that he was much too close! The force of the truck striking against the front side of her car threw her car out of control, forcing it to veer to the right suddenly. She felt her car going air-bound and out of control. She braced herself and hung onto the steering wheel tightly as her car plummeted down the embankment. She screamed, feeling helpless as her car careened out of control and narrowly missed big oak trees as the vehicle bounced out of control. The hillside was steep, and the car tumbled and managed to break through low hanging branches. As if it tripped, it then somersaulted end over end the rest of the way down the embankment into the water. There was nothing she could do but hang on and ride it out. She screamed as the car bounced and tumbled down the embankment until it splashed into the murky water. The car got hung up on fallen branches and other debris and quickly sunk to the muddy, soft bottom of the flooded field. The whole area had become a lake with all the heavy downpours the site had been receiving almost every day for the past month. She thanked the universe for safely helping get her out of the wreckage and crawl back up onto the roadway.

Margo felt numb as she laid alone on the wet, dark roadway; she thought perhaps she would see the big black pickup truck parked along that stretch of road with someone there looking to help her. But there was no one; neither the driver nor the car was anywhere in sight. How could someone possibly knowing they had caused an accident just drive off. She looked down toward the water she had just emerged from, and in the light of the full moon, she could see the rear end undercarriage of her car sticking out of the water; so sure if that truck ended up in the water too, she would have seen it as it was a much larger vehicle than her car.

So she knew the driver must have driven off. It all had happened so fast; she only recalled it being a truck, a big black pickup truck. She knew she would never forget the sight of those bright red taillights moving fast away as she careened down the embankment toward the dark water. It would be etched in her brain forever. She could only think that it had been an accident, for it was far too challenging to consider and ponder the idea that someone would deliberately hit her car with the sheer intend of forcing her car off the road. Whoever was driving the truck had to see in their rearview mirror bouncing headlights careening off the road; that is if they even bothered to look. Was the driver drunk? Why didn't the driver stop after he struck her car? Instead, the driver raced away from the scene, leaving her for dead. Why?

Chapter Three

Margo was amazed and very thankful that she had somehow managed to pull herself up the steep embankment. She was exhausted and laid in a muddy mess along the side of the roadway. She laid there for what seemed a long time to catch her breath and come to terms with what had just happened. Margo knew she was in shock when she saw the blinding bright light above her and thought: *Well, here I go again another near-death experience.* There was that time when she had gone to the bright sunlight. It was beautiful and wonderful. She wanted to stay, but her spirit guides had sent her back to earth. They had told her it was not yet her time. She wondered, *was this the end of her time now?*

Margo stared up in disbelief at the sudden appearance of a very bright light shining down, surrounding her in a warm glow. The light was so bright she had to shield her eyes. After what she had just survived, she was not afraid but just curious and wondered what was going on. She was so tired and too weak to struggle or worry. As she laid there, she looked up and saw that there was some sort of craft hovering above her. It was huge, circular, and silent. Its satiny, silver finish glowed in the moonlight. She laid there gazing up in amazement. She was mesmerized. Suddenly, as if in a dream, she felt lifted, weightless, and as light as a feather. She felt her body rise higher and higher, gently rising until she was taken up into the light source. Why start being afraid now, for she had just faced possible death being sideswiped by the truck and forced off the road. She had been trapped and nearly drowned and yet managed to get herself out of an almost wholly submerged vehicle. Miraculously, Margo never felt alone throughout the whole ordeal. She always felt that there was an exceptional magical power guiding and helping her. She had no idea the source of the bright light. Did she have another near-death experience, she wondered? No, this time was much different. This time the bright light came down from a silent round circular craft of some sort.

Was it the Pleiadians she had often read about? She was not afraid but instead suddenly felt a sense of great curiosity along with a sense of spiritual connectedness. She read whatever she could about the Pleiadians because these otherworldly beings somehow resonated with her. Margo was introduced to them and became even more interested when she happened across a lecture at a local bookstore. The speaker spoke of the Age of Aquarius Fifth Dimension arrival of the feminine Pleiadian influence. He explained that the Pleiadians came from the Pleiades star cluster in the Taurus constellation. The Pleiadians were the benevolent feminine rulers of the Fifth Dimension Age of Aquarius. The material of the lecture resonated and stayed with her. It was as if she belonged to them and came from the Pleiades. As soon as she heard the word: Pleiadian, she had felt that she was a Pleiadian from the Pleiades star cluster in the Taurus constellation. The more she read about the Pleiadians and the Pleiades star system, the more she thought it was where she came from and would return to again one day.

The craft had silently hovered above Margo. Its huge bright antigravity lights had shown down upon her. Surprisingly, Margo was not afraid. Instead, she felt a certain familiar warmth about the lights that she could not explain. The antigravity effect made it possible for Margo to defy gravity, as she magically rose high from the ground and then miraculously appeared in the craft. In awe and amazement, she felt warm and safe, and then as if it were just too much for her to handle, she passed out.

She was unconscious for a moment, or so, it seemed anyway, and when she awoke, she found herself lying on a soft, comfortable cot. She looked around the craft and at herself. To her wonder and amazement, she was all cleaned up and felt dry, warm, and comfortable. She looked down and saw that she was wearing a warm and comfortable silver-colored soft material one-piece outfit like a jumpsuit. She looked around in amazement at her surroundings. It appeared to her that she was in some sort of spacecraft. The craft seemed very futuristic, with sleek styling control panels that surrounded the pilot and copilot control stations. Looking out from small portal-style windows that encircled the ship, Margo could see the stars and her old friend, the moon. Seeing the moon brought comfort to her. She felt overwhelmed with gratitude and love. The whole experience was so surreal that she indeed wondered if she had died.

She was convinced she had passed on to the other side and was ready to accept that fact; when she saw a beautiful woman appear before her. The woman had long blonde hair and large green almond-shaped eyes. The lovely woman smiled warmly and stood before Margo as she laid on the cot. Margo felt strangely safe in her presence and her extraordinary otherworldly surroundings. The mysterious woman smiled, and Margo felt wrapped in the warmth of ever-encompassing love. The woman appeared heavenly, and Margo was astonished and marveled at the beauty standing before her. She felt the warmth and love radiate out from the aura of this lovely being. A sense of rising curiosity and excitement rose within her. She wanted to learn more.

"Where am I?" Margo finally asked after a few seconds, looking up into the woman's mesmerizingly eyes.

"You are safe in our craft up amongst the stars and the planets," the lovely woman reported in a soft, soothing voice that was comforting to Margo even in this fantastic otherworldly setting.

"Did I die?" Margo finally asked in a weak voice just above a whisper.

"No, you did not die, my dear, " answered the lovely lady in a sweet loving voice.

Margo was surprised that she was not afraid. Instead, she felt the loving, peaceful calm of the atmosphere of where she was and the lovely woman before her. She felt safe and warm, as if she were wrapped in loving arms. She no longer felt fear and pain, only the sense of warmth and unconditional love.

"Who are you, and where am I?" asked Margo intrigued, for she knew the being standing before her had to be from another planet.

"My name is Sara, and this is my spacecraft," she said proudly and proceeded to explain, "I am the Commander of this craft. We onboard this craft are from Alcyone.

"Tell me about Alcyone," pressed Margo, anxious to learn more.

"Alcyone is the brightest star of seven sister stars that make up the Pleiades star cluster in the Taurus constellation. Alcyone is where you are from, originally," explained Sara.

"I am?" asked Margo with a puzzled look. "I thought I was from Earth."

"Yes, you were born on Earth as a volunteer human and Pleiadian hybrid from Alcyone," offered Sara.

"Who in their right mind would volunteer to go to Earth?" responded Margo, feeling surprised but very comfortable and safe.

"I get your point, but yes, you did volunteer," confirmed the tall, slender blonde, her green eyes twinkling.

"Why don't I know that I am from Alcyone, as you say?" asked Margo.

"Because part of the promise of the journey to learn from and help human beings is to forget the details of the path you have chosen to take. Because before you were born on Earth, you volunteered to be born on Earth as a Pleiadian and human hybrid to help humankind transform from the Annunaki Reptilian Age of Pisces of the Fourth Dimension into the feminine Pleiadian rule of the Age of Aquarius of the Fifth Dimension of love, harmony, and understanding. It is happening now as Earth moves from a rather destructive Anunnaki Reptilian male authoritarian patriarchal rule into the uplifting feminine power, the loving tradition of building and reconstructing love around the world."

"I feel like I am dreaming," stated Margo feeling almost overwhelmed, "why would I volunteer to go to such an awful place like Earth? The planet of self-serving, enslaving of all others by the male patriarchal authoritarian rule. These people work solely for a handful of greedy big corporate heads who are wealthy political contributors. All of this lobbying has made a mess of our democracy. All the gerrymandering the conservatives do to keep the poor minorities from voting and having their votes counted. If these atrocities are allowed to continue, I fear we will lose our democracy to a dictatorship. The conservative government has tried in every way to remove or privatize every tax supportive social benefit just for their selfish profits. It's so depressing to see," remarked Margo.

"We are well aware of the difficulties presenting themselves in your country on the planet Earth," Sara noted in a more serious tone.

"Don't get me wrong, " stated Margo, "Earth itself is a beautiful place, and once upon a time, everything we needed in the way of food, healing herbs, and plants were here. Life would be perfect if there were not greedy morons of Anunnaki Reptilian decent, disguised as humans, making a mess of things. Too bad they do not appreciate this beautiful planet." Margo said with a sad look on her face.

"Yes, earthly Anunnaki Reptilian bred humans have a way of messing up a good thing," agreed Sara. She saw the look of curiosity on Margo's face and added. "I'm sure you have more questions."

"I do have many more questions. So, I am a Pleiadian human hybrid, you say," asked Margo. She wanted to be sure she got it right.

"Yes," confirmed Sara.

"Well then, maybe that is why I have such a difficult time trying to understand the human mentality, especially the male mentality," explained Margo, "I have read many books on the subject of nasty Anunnaki Reptilian creatures from Mars who ruined their planet by being greedy and reckless, so they evacuated Mars and came to inhabit planet Earth." Margo continued with her rant, "it appears to me that there is an elitist power group behind both political parties that directs and pulls strings in the federal government and that their mission is to divide, conquer and dominate the populations not only of the United States but of the world, and their end goal is a single New World Order dictatorship," stated Margo.

"You are right on point, my dear," smiled Sara and added, "you may be more intuitive and psychic than you think."

"It appears to me that they want us fighting with each other to divide, conquer, and destroy Democracy. Because united we stand, divided we fall. It is so sad to me that so many Americans do not see this. And that fact in itself is slowly destroying the freedom of life, in every sense, on planet Earth," said Margo.

"Being on planet Earth can be is so disturbing," complained Margo, "will it ever get better?" Margo knew firsthand that life could be challenging as she had lived in fear of her husband, Jack, who was mean and cruel.

"Yes, it can get better, and you are going to help usher in the Age of Aquarius, the Fifth Dimension," declared Sara.

"How could I possibly help people on Earth?" asked Margo. "How can I help women to wise up and rise up, and get out from under authoritarian men's misogynistic rule?"

"You have already helped," said Sara with a smile, "by paying attention to national and worldly affairs. The energy of your positive quantum thoughts along with everyone else's goes out into the universe, and realities are changed."

"I had no idea," remarked Margo listening intently to what Sara had to say.

"Spiritual beings on Earth as human beings are part of the whole universal consciousness," said Sara. "In other words, we are all connected. If only we would allow ourselves to believe it. Thoughts create change. Love creates love. Hate creates more hate that gets implanted in our minds. Unfortunately, males bear the brunt of this as males still are and have been brought up to be rough and tough and ready for war. And being descendants of Reptilian Anunnaki Martian rule, males are easy to manipulate and brainwashed into thinking that they are superior, especially Aryan white males--who, as self-proclaimed creations of excellence, prevail at the top rung of white supremacy. According to the Anunnaki rule, white males of the Aryan race were put on Earth to enslave all other races and the opposite sex. In a way, men are indeed the victims of the Fourth Dimension Anunnaki Reptilian rule as they unknowingly became the evil slaves, tricked into thinking they were superior," explained Sara.

"That doesn't sound good at all," feared Margo, "because they are not superior above all-overs. "

"You are so right, my dear," confirmed Sara and added. "Women are rising in every profession and surpassing males in every area of intellectual development. More women are entering and completing college degrees than men. More women are starting up new businesses, becoming doctors, lawyers, professors, and corporate heads. Women have surpassed men in every area of society," said Sara. "It will be women who straighten out the mess that is in your country at this time."

"Do you think men thought women were superior from the get-go, and that is why they took every effort to hold them back?" Margo wondered.

"Yes, I agree they fear women as threats to their manhood. Men feel they must dominate in order to overcome insecurities. Men by design are most favored for occupations of laborer and soldiering," smiled Sara.

"Tell me more," asked Margo.

"Men like to push through challenges to win, making them feel strong, successful, and manly. They make great laborers of simple tasks. In ancient times Martians came to Earth from Mars to mine the gold that was loaded up and rocketed back to Mars. This gold dust was used to try to save the atmosphere on Mars. As all their greedy activities robbed Mars of all its capability of keeping Mars a healthy living planet."

"So now the greedy, reckless ones are here on Earth to use it up to serve their greed and ruin it with their competitive warlike behavior," deducted Margo.

"I'm afraid so," Sara sadly had to agree.

"I don't think I can change all of that. So, therefore, I don't want to be on Earth," begged Margo.

"Well, you may have to be, but I am here to help

you," Sara was about to say that Margo chooses her path's level of difficulty and seems she bit off more than she could chew, and that was why Sara was there to help her.

"I want to go with you back to Alcyone. You say I am from Alcyone, then take me there with you, Sara."

Sara was happy in a way that Margo wanted to come back home to Alcyone. Sara was Margo's Pleiadian guardian and overseer while she was on Earth. It was Sara's job to make sure that Margo was safe while performing her duties on planet Earth as a Pleiadian hybrid volunteer. As Margo was born on planet Earth, she was unaware or had forgotten her mission and the reason she incarnated to earth. Unbeknownst to Margo until now, to learn she had taken upon herself her chosen project, to help humans prepare to raise from the fourth to the Fifth Dimension of higher vibrational frequencies and consciousness in this the dawning of the Age of Aquarius.

Sara learned that many human Pleiadian hybrids even though they volunteered to come to Earth, find that when they do, they do not like being on Earth. They do not like it here, it is too barbaric, so they choose to live alone and not marry or have children. For to do so would create karma, and they do not want to need to return to Earth to live out that karma. Pleiadian hybrids are soul healers and psychic empaths. They feel what others are feeling and that explains why many Pleiadian hybrids prefer to live alone. Because sometimes all those emotions can be overbearing. Sara knew to handle Margo gently because what she was feeling was very common among the Pleiadian hybrids. So Sara understood why hybrids wanted to return to Alcyone.

Chapter Four

Life on the Pleiades' brightest star, Alcyone, is far more advanced than life on Earth as Margo had known it. Alcyone is such a wonderful place with a spiritual loving atmosphere. No hate exists there, no greed exists there, no illness exists there, no wars exist there, no poverty exists there, only love and harmony, and good will for one another. The positive energy that envelopes the star cluster enhances positive loving energy that rises up and permeates throughout the universe. Sara knew that the residences of Alcyone were far more advanced intellectually and emotionally than the human beings on planet Earth. Alcyone residents possessed super high technology in all forms and could either use their voices to speak to one another or communicate telepathically by directing and sending thoughts to another.

Alcyone is mystical and magical. It is so perfect and those residing there are sad to see the terrible Anunnaki Reptilian barbaric behavior of racism, war mongers, greed, narcissism, and authoritarian patriarchal rule that existed on planet Earth. They want to help to save the planet. But according to galactic rule, the Pleiadians were not to appear on planet Earth to help directly. They could only observe. It was an order difficult to obey and a few insisted not to obey, such as Sara and her crew on Sara's silver saucer who found ways around that galactic rule. To get around past the rule, some would voluntarily be born as human and Pleiadian hybrids on planet Earth. Margo had chosen to do just that. But to her dismay, she soon found out that the job would be very difficult. Margo was disappointed when she realized human beings on Earth were proven to be more barbaric in their ways of greed and distrust compared to peaceful and loving beings of Alcyone.

Margo did not like growing up on Earth and living in a patriarchal society where she felt men, especially white men, out ranked everyone else, and all women were put in secondary positions as helpless creatures best suited for bearing children, cooking, cleaning, and honoring and obeying the patriarchal ruler of the family.

Margo's job was very difficult because there were good and bad among human beings living on earth. Margo's husband, Jack, turned out to be one of the bad ones. In Margo's experience, it was mostly patriarchal authoritarian groups led by white males who were the disrupters of progress for most Americans. The country was socially brainwashed to put non- whites and women of all races in secondary social positions.

Men wrote the rules so the powers they established were created to suit themselves. They thought they were gods. They were very competitive, they clawed and cheated their way up the rungs of corporate and political ladders with whatever it took,. Even when it came to the Bible, Margo was convinced that human males wrote the living world in the bibles to fit their agenda, needs, taste, and desires. Margo thought a real god would have created all living souls to be equal, and not make white men superior. But men created the rules and laws to serve themselves and they put themselves above everyone else, by enslaving women and persons of color. They wanted loyalty and servitude by fellow humans, so they chose to designate women and people of color as lesser valued beings. Men wrote the social rules and religious commandments that considered women to be slaves like second-class citizens of docile servitude to love, honor, and obey their men. It was the men who raised their social status well above the others and established themselves as the leaders, warriors, and the more intelligent and stronger gender. Years ago in the 1950s, women wore pearls and house dresses, and men wore suits and tipped their hats and opened doors for them, at least chivalry was alive and well, in public anyway.

It was difficult to be your true self when there were gender rolls and social rules. Margo didn't stand a chance of freedom to be herself between the strict patriarchal doctrine of the church and strict religious centered instructions at school. Her parents were deeply involved in the men's and women's organizations of the church. Catholics girls were handed prayer books that instructed them how to act. They were taught to be obedient and docile, seen and not heard, and to listen to and honor all authority figures. Margo was primed from little up; she was told as a small child that boys were raised to be adventurous, that they were smarter than girls, and boys were favored more to be the first child to carry on the family name.

None of the males designed social standards to be followed by boys and girls set well for Margo. She was abused as a child. She had no recourse when her uncle sexually abused her. She told her mother, who did not believe her and appeared to make light of it. Her mother told her not to tell her father as it would upset him too much. So Margo thought she did the next best thing and told the priest in the confessional. It did not take long for Margo to realize that that was a huge mistake. The perverted priest set up her penitence as private counseling sessions in the church's vestibule, with him, alone. There he had her cornered and took advantage of the situation by also molesting her. Sara knew Margo's history and it was one of the reasons why she came to Earth to help her. Something had to be done to stop the patriarchal authoritarian misogynistic abuse against women and children.

Self-serving men were everywhere. They paved their own way to serve their own greed and gain riches by cheating and stealing from others. Some politicians and those in high corporate positions found ways to rip off the so-called middle class which as a result was slipping further and further into poverty. It would only take the expense of one emergency, one injury or illness, to lose their livelihood and life savings and slip into poverty and homelessness. It seemed to Margo that the conservative side of government did nothing to help the slipping away middle class; but rather it appeared to Margo that they catered to the wealthiest corporate donors which were the cause of the social economic divide in this country by keeping tax-break money for themselves and by failing trickle-down economic efforts.

Margo had trouble trying to figure it all out. She only thought that being on Earth was a very frustrating place to be and it gave her a feeling of hopelessness. To her, it seemed the white European male descendants were so intent on dominance and power, that they invaded and massacred native Americans and sold their land and stole their country. White males placed themselves above all others and set the rules. Men set the rules, so of course catered the rules to suit themselves thereby making themselves masters above all others. All others were set-up for servitude positions.

Aside from that, Margo wondered if there was a grand scheme to things. She wondered if there was a behind-the-scenes elite group, or secret society, that controlled everything done regarding federal government and its direction to the actions of both parties. In other words, were secret cabal groups, pulling the strings of the actions of both parties? Margo paid attention to what was going on across the country and was frustrated with all the discrepancy, racist and political turmoil. She felt as if she did not belong in all the chaos that surrounded her on Earth. It was too much for her. Margo was an empath and took on every emotion of every wrong doing. She was happy for Sara's spacecraft escape.

So Margo found herself happy to be on the spaceship and away from the seemly barbaric happenings on earth. She sat up on the cot to get a better look. She looked around in delight at her wondrous magical surroundings. Everything was so peaceful, organized, and very futuristic.

Margo soon discovered that there were several other beings moving about on the spacecraft. Although they were out of sight, Margo could sense their presence as they appeared to be moving about performing various tasks. It appeared to her that they went about their business operating the craft as it maneuvered throughout space, although no dials, buttons or levers were seen to be operated. Margo wondered just how did they fly the spacecraft. But she was not frightened nor concerned about her present whereabouts. Instead, she was happy to see that there was indeed a reality beyond Earth that appeared peaceful and loving unlike the dog-eat-dog competitiveness of where Margo was from.

From a portal near where she sat up on the cot, Margo could see stars and the full moon which in her mind appeared to be smiling back at her. Her old buddy the moon. It appeared to be very close. Margo was happy to see her old friend, as she did when she laid trapped in the over-turned car. Feeling the moon's glow again gave her hope. The sense of time seemed to have been altered and the accident seemed to have happened a long time ago. Margo felt healed, safe and warm in this sleek ultra-futuristic silent craft as it darted about the universe. She felt warm and protected. Again, Margo repeated her previous question.

"Where am I?" Margo asked feeling rather surprised that she was not afraid.

"You, my dear, are in a spacecraft of your peers," smiled the beauty looking at her as Margo sat on a small soft cot.

"My peers?" Margo asked with wide eyes. Was she dreaming, she wondered.

"Yes, my dear," smiled the beauty, "with your peers."

"Am I dead, did I die?" asked Margo in a concerned voice.

"No, you are very much alive," replied the ageless beauty before her, "we rescued you and brought you here to heal your wounds."

"You sure I did not die?" questioned Margo, "I have had a near-death experiences before. The first one was about three years ago, when my husband beat me so severely that if the neighbors, hearing what was going on, had not called the police and an ambulance, I know I would have surely died. As it was, I was in intensive care for a week and in a coma for three of those days." She was rambling, maybe she was a little nervous after all.

"We are well aware of your beatings by your Earth husband and your near-death experiences," exclaimed Sara.

"You are?" asked Margo with a tone of surprise to her voice.

"We helped heal you and kept you on planet Earth" admitted Sara.

"Why?" asked Margo, "Earth is so barbaric."

"You did not die then when he beat you, and you did not die now when you were forced off the road and your car landed upside down in the water," explained Sara.

"Was it my jerk of a husband, Jack," exclaimed Margo, "who forced me off the road?"

"I am afraid so, my dear," answered Sara.

"You sure I am not dead, because this feels very much like a some kind of dream state," Margo wanted to know.

"No my dear, you did not die, you are very much alive," smiled Sara.

"So I am a Pleiadian like you?" Margo asked with confused wide eyed curiosity.

"Yes, Margo. I am a Pleiadian, just as you are. You hit your head pretty hard in the crash and that is why you do not recall that you are a hybrid, both Pleiadian and human. You are a blue star seed from the Pleiades. There are many of you on planet Earth. And one way that humans on Earth can become aware that they are from the Pleiades is to learn about your Astrology Natal Birth Chart. All humans who have the sun, moon, North or South node, or any of the planets in the sign of Taurus in their Astrological Birth Chart is a Pleiadian. For they are indeed volunteer Pleiadian hybrid helpers born on Earth from the Pleiades star system located in the Taurus constellation. Like the others, you are on earth to help those who are suffering from all the earth's negative energy. You are on earth to help prepare humans for the feminine Pleiadian rule of the Age of Aquarius and the Fifth Dimension. And for the future of higher consciousness, the dawning of harmony, peace, love and understanding on Earth. The greedy, lawless, underhanded ideals of the male oriented Fourth Dimension Reptilian Anunnaki rule is nearing the end of its reign. And then they will be gone, as they cannot survive in the loving feminine rule of the Age of Aquarius Fifth Dimension.

One by one the human minds in your country alone will be enlightened by your light-minded collective thoughts. People around you feel your special otherworldly energy and therefore beseech your help as the population evolves and enters into the Fifth Dimension of higher consciousness." Sara shared as Margo listened with wide eyed interest.

"Well, life on earth, certainly could use all the positive help and energy it can get," said Margo feeling very concerned and willing to help however she could. Margo often wondered what man would do after they make planet Earth uninhabitable. Will they go back to Mars? But, they have already ruined planet Mars which was once green and habitable much like Earth is now, well is now, for the time being. Margo suspected many have already reserved their seat in the space module that is taking reservations for a one way ticket to Mars for encapsulated modular living.

"We can only watch Earth's debacle from afar because according to Galactic rule we cannot interfere in Earth's activities, that is, in plain sight. We do however have ways around that," Sara informed Margo.

"Is that a fact?" Margo was interested in learning more.

"Hybrids can be birthed onto earth to fit right in with human lifestyles. Their purpose is to help prepare and move civilization onward into the Fifth Dimension and by the rising feminine energy of the Fifth Dimension change for the better will come. The negative male egotistical and narcissistic Anunnaki and Reptilian warlike dominance will eventually cease because they cannot survive beyond the fourth dimension. They were on Earth originally throughout ancient history, because genetically seeded descendants from various planets have manifested on Earth, some benevolent, some not so benevolent," explained Sara.

"What is the Fifth Dimension all about?" Margo wanted to know.

"The Fifth Dimension is about healing. The Fourth Dimension Anunnaki Reptilian descendants caused all the evil greed, wars for profit, millions of shootings, and white-collar crimes on earth. Eventually, they will cease to exist as they will grow old and die out. The generations that follow will correct and reverse the negativity of the old ways that harmed the environment. They will make way for cleaner advanced technologies, which will be one of the much-needed advances made to help save the planet. Only then will the Earth be rejuvenated. In no time at all, the old ways of the Age of Pisces, the Fourth Dimension way of doing things, that proved negative to the life of the planet and its inhabitants will be cast to the wayside. In the age of Aquarius, racism and gender bias will be gone as races and gender becomes more androgynous and blending in their appearances. As we leave the Fourth Dimension behind and as a result of being in the Age of Aquarius Fifth Dimension, males in particular will become more sensitive to how their actions affect others. Most women are already in the feminist Pleiadian rule Age of Aquarius; they have been waiting for the males to catch up with them intellectually and emotionally and to lose the need to dominate," explained Sara.

"Hearing all that, I look forward to the future," said Margo smiling with her green eyes wide with wonder. Margo knew all too well who they were as she had experience in real-time the all-white male dominance in society. Patriarchal authoritarian rule had dominated all of society. Men always paid themselves more and designated and labeled jobs specifically for either men or women. Women's specific jobs were librarian, nurse, teacher, store clerk, hotel maid, childcare, and restaurant worker. Men set it up so they made more money than women, men controlled the money and kept women locked in lessor paying positions, for no reason Margo could see, but to keep women in their place and to be discriminated against as secondary citizens. Men had to feel powerful and be in control. Margo had deducted from what she witnessed in her everyday life and read in the newspapers and heard on the news. Margo felt, that like herself, there were more wives who were emotionally beaten down intentionally so they would not have the self-esteem and confidence to try to leave the relationship and strike out on her own.

"It appears that there is a secret society of greedy powerful ones who seek dictatorships and power to eventually rule the whole Western Hemisphere and divide the world into two empires, East and West. Two dictatorships. To one day fight each other until it comes down to a total of one, the New World Order global empire. This is what could happen, and it would subsequently destroy the planet. Its why we Pleiadians had to intervene somehow," explained Sara.

"Please tell me more," begged Margo wanting to learn all she could.

"According to galactic rule, we cannot openly present ourselves to Earth's population by appearing in a craft above the White House or the Capitol of the country by making a grand entrance. We cannot interfere openly. But we can birth hybrids into the Earth's population to hopefully aid mankind into evolving," explained Sara.

"So how on Earth can I possibly help?" asked Margo feeling a bit too tired right then to do much of anything. But in that moment she meant the full intent of her comment, she did want to help.

"Anunnaki Reptilian Age of Pisces and the Fourth Dimension evil patriarchal rule has overrun planet Earth since Sumerian days; that is after the feminine power of Atlantis was overcome by authoritarian patriarchal rule. Warlike, authoritarian selfish evil greed has continued for centuries and if left to continue on in the same manner will eventually destroy planet Earth," said Sara.

Margo understood that there was now renewed promise of hope for planet Earth and its inhabitants as Earth enters the Fifth Dimension and the Age of Aquarius with feminine Pleiadians rule.

"It's time for universal change and it is occurring now. The days of authoritarian rule are ending. Patriarchal, authoritarian, tumultuous rule will end as its the ending of the Anunnaki Reptilian rule of the Pisces fourth dimension. We have entered the dawning of the Pleiadian, guardians of the planet, feminine rule of the fifth dimension, the age of Aquarius. The human condition needs to move from fear of people's differences to unconditional love for one another. This is where Pleiadian hybrids, such as yourself, come into play. Love brings love. Loving thoughts and actions create more loving thoughts and actions," explained Sara.

"Just who are Reptilians and Anunnaki and where do they come from?" asked Margo suddenly full of questions.

"Reptilians and Anunnaki races are noxious energies cast off planet Mars. They used it, abused it and destroyed any possibility of living on that planet. Mars was once as green and full of life as Earth, but Anunnaki Reptilian egotistical competitive greed destroyed life on Mars, so they migrated to planet Earth. And now oddly enough they are super wealthy and are building space directed missiles to deliver accommodating modules to live in on Mars. They will live in modules until they can determine if there is any trace of the necessary atmosphere that is needed in order to openly live on Mars; which was once possible in the ancient alien past. Like homing pigeons, the Martian Anunnaki, Reptilians want to return to their home planet of Mars. In Ancient alien times, as the short story goes, they needed gold dust to try to restore their thinning atmosphere that an invading reptilian meteor had nearly destroyed. The Martians were tired of mining the gold on Earth themselves, so they created slaves from those cast out. The reptilian slaves sent to Earth to work mated with the females on Earth," explained Sara.

"Knowing that now, makes it so frightening to know evil Anunnaki Reptilian ones are here and will do the same to planet Earth as they did to Mars," said Margo with a worrisome tone to her voice. She listened as Sara explained more.

Thus you have the greedy evil Anunnaki Reptilian mentalities of the higher-ups ruling over corporation heads and politicians," explained Sara.

"That's a lot to take in," Margo was entranced.

"I know that is a lot of information," stated Sara, "but I have a feeling you are already fairly well aware of most of what I stated."

"Yes I am aware," Margo sadly admitted, "it still doesn't make it any easier to live with though."

Chapter Five

Margo's Astrological natal birth sun sign is Taurus. Taurus is a fixed Earth sign. So a home-body type, prefers normalcy and therefore slow to make any kind of changes. She fit her sun sign to a tee, as no matter how difficult the situation, she desired stability and the security of what she thought marriage should be, no matter how unhappy. For better or for worse it's what one does. Margo came from a long legacy of obstinate women. It's what her mother did and her mother before her. They stuck it out till the end no matter how awful the marriage was because to be divorced in the eyes of the church was far worse and divorcees were seen as "loose" women and ostracized from married social groups.

As her Taurus traits revealed, Margo was slow to make change, all along though, she realized that she needed to leave Jack at some point; but change proved to be difficult for Margo. Having to act on her own needed secure fashion, she knew she stayed in the marriage much too long. But she also sensed that she had to find a safe exit and a secure shelter before she ever seriously thought about leaving and divorcing Jack. His behavior was getting worse, she needed to hurry with that plan, and she knew it.

Margo could see evidence of the Anunnaki Reptilian Aryan male brain in her husband, Jack; boy could she. She saw his temper and the evil look in his eyes when he was angry and yelled at her. She was frightened as she realized all too well the horrible things he was capable of doing.

Margo had seen Jack's egotistical and narcissistic male lawless ways. And all she had do was to read the headlines of the newspapers and watch the evening news on television to see this was true of many men.

Chapter Six

"What do I need to do?" Margo suddenly felt energized at the thought of being in service for the higher good of all humankind. Margo had always felt other worldly and now she knew why. It was because she was a Pleiadian hybrid from Alcyone, the brightest and central star of the Pleiades star system located in the constellation of Taurus. She was a Pleiadian hybrid, born on earth to aid human progress into the higher elevation of consciousness feminine rule of the Pleiadians, here now to help humans advance into the Fifth Dimension of the age of Aquarius.

"You are a soul healer, so mingle, join activists' groups," Sara said in a sweet voice. "Because your earthly magnetic presence is enough for all those who come into contact with you to rise to a higher elevation of consciousness. They will become prepared to shift to a higher consciousness that is occurring now with the dawning of the Age of Aquarius. It is a time when humans rise up to the Fifth Dimension as they are enlightened."

"Even Jack driving the truck that sideswiped me and forced me down the steep embankment into the freezing water?" Margo asked. "He certainly came into contact with me."

"Yes, Jack believe it or not, knows he is a Anunnaki Reptilian moron, although not in those exact terms. He has already begun to feel slight remorse for what he has done but its fading fast, as he is weak in his soul consciousness. And his bad behavior will continue," Sara shared.

"Why did he do it?" asked Margo needing to know why the man she married had turned into an evil doer.

"Your husband Jack, I'm sorry to say, ran you off the road that evening in order to collect life insurance money from the policy he took out on you,"

"That rat," sighed Margo she could not believe what she was hearing.

"Oh yes," declared Sara.

"Unbelievable," stated Margo, "just what kind of hidden monster did I marry?"

"Your husband took out a large dollar value life insurance policy on you when he learned from your mutual friend, Joe, that you were thinking of divorcing him."

"You must be kidding," questioned Margo, "how did Joe know? I did not speak to Joe about my plans to divorce Jack."

"Joe overheard you speaking to your friend Claire

about getting a divorce from Jack. Unfortunately, before you got a chance to file the divorce papers, Joe slipped and mentioned something to Jack. But Jack already had his plans for your demise in place. His goal was to collect the life insurance policy he had taken out on you. You are his third marriage, and he has had high value life insurance policies on his two previous wives, who are unfortunately deceased."

"What?" Margo was astonished by the news of her husband's plan for her demise for monetary reasons.

"He wanted to end your life in order to collect the money before you could divorce him and get half of everything he had," stated Sara.

"The audacity," stated Margo! Margo thought her husband, Jack, loved her but now things, like his recent erratic temperament, were beginning to make sense. It struck a chord of fear within her. She recalled the way she met Jack and in retrospect it did appear suspiciously convenient on his part.

Chapter Seven

Margo had met Jack one day when he stopped to help fix her flat tire. He was following right behind her so pulled over when he saw she had a flat tire. The nice tall, tan, handsome man with sandy colored hair blowing in the breeze walked up to her open window and introduced himself. He bent down slightly to talk to her. He wore kakis and a long sleeve white shirt with a loosened necktie. He was very kind and offered to change the tire for her. As he loosened the bolts then jacked up the car, he told her he was a widower and that his wife had died of cancer. He seemed like a nice guy and she enjoyed talking to him.

She was driving a new Lexus she bought for herself after receiving very generous commission bonus for being the top salesman in the agency. She had sold several multi-million-dollar homes. Her commission and bonus earnings were enough for her to retire; that is, if she invested smartly and managed it well, which she was doing. Her hard work had paid off.

And then there was Jack. Unlike Margo, he had a more creative way of making money. Jack collected life insurance money on his deceased wives. Margo's way of making money was hard work and dedicated discipline, while Jack's money making strategies were sinister and evil as unsuspecting women became his victims. Potential victim number three was Margo when he so coincidentally, just happened to be following her when she got the flat tire.

"Oh yes, I am sorry to say, my dear, that he had this little episode planned from the time he read the article about your real estate selling success in the local paper, and he was determined to meet you," Sara informed Margo with a sympathetic tone to her voice.

"That is very interesting all right, as I thought it was very convenient that he happened to show up just at the moment I realized I had a flat tire and pulled over to the side of the road," recalled Margo. "I thought I was so fortunate to have someone stop to help me. I had just pulled out of the subdivision after showing a couple of large high-priced homes located on a gated golf course community development on the edge of town. Now that I recall, there was not much traffic. I recall I earlier saw his car parked on the same street, he was also driving a Lexus which I believe is why I noticed it," recalled Margo with a serious look about her as she recalled passed events that led up to her present predicament. She realized then that Jack had sabotaged her car, puncturing her tire so he could come to her rescue.

"Well, there you have it," said Sara, "now you know

why and how he planned to meet you, and that was
by setting up a situation where he could come to your
rescue.

Chapter Eight

"So, more about Jack another time," commanded Margo returning her attention to the present and looking around the craft. "I want to learn more about you, and this craft. For starters, do I call you captain?" asked Margo of the lovely lady who miraculously came to her rescue, got her cleaned up and healed her cuts and bruises.

"You can call me Sara, you and I need not be formal, but keep in mind that I am the captain of this ship," replied Sara proudly, a twinkle in her clear green eyes, "and my all-girl crew address me as Captain."

"Captain," smiled Margo, "I'm impressed, I would be happy to address you as 'Captain.'"

"Please call me by my name. Sara, that would be good," Sara replied.

"Then Sara it is," smiled Margo.

"And what would you like to be called, my dear?" asked Sara with a smile.

"'Pilot in training' would be nice," Margo answered

and they both laughed. Indeed she was in a craft above all other crafts. So futuristic, there was nothing like it on planet Earth as far as Margo knew. She instantly liked Sara and her crew. She felt comfortable and at home being with Sara.

It felt good to laugh once again, if only for a moment. Sara went on to show Margo around her silver saucer, which was a craft above all others, certainly above anything Margo had seen. The craft was silent, nimble, bullet-fast and could become invisible to the human eye. Sara explained a few things to Margo about herself. She said that she was a Pleiadian overseer and as a full-pledged Pleiadian, she could appear and disappear anywhere without the transport of the craft if she chose to do so. In other words, for Sara, the craft was mainly for show.

"So what do you think about us and the craft so far?" asked Sara with a smile at the wide-eyed woman sitting up now and looking all about. She could tell Margo was full of curiosity about her and the magnificent circular silver craft she controlled that darted about across space and time.

"I think it is magical and you are magical and mystical," sighed Margo. "I am so happy to be with you."

"Likewise," agreed Sara.

Chapter Nine

"So, what happens now?" Margo asked Sara. "Will you continue to help me? I sure could use more help because when I return to my home and Jack realizes that I am alive, my life will for sure be in danger."

"We are here to help you and guide you," assured Sara.

"What do I do about my horrible husband?" Margo asked. "What will happen to me?"

"If he finds out that you are alive, he will try to kill you again, of course," smiled Sara, "but there is nothing for you to fear."

"There isn't?" asked Margo. "That's good to hear, but just the same, I am a Pleiadian human hybrid, so I do feel fear."

This was hard for Margo to take in and try to understand. First of all, she felt like a fool being a victim of her husband. She was an intelligent woman so she felt that she should have known better and should have seen it coming. She always wondered how he made his money, because he always had plenty of it. When she asked, he always said that he was a day trader and lucky with his investments. Of course, Margo knew nothing about day trading, so she trusted whatever he told her. She had no reason not to believe him. Margo thought that he was quit the catch. He was a good looking man with lots of charm and easily won her over soon after they met. And now to find out he made his money deceiving and murdering his wives made the little hairs in the back of her neck stand up. She felt used and abused but fortunate to be alive. She felt like a fool, having fallen under Jack's charming spell. Jack was the most charming man she had ever met. He was polite and kind when he pulled over behind her to help her with the flat tire on her car. Little did she know that he had punctured her tire just so he could follow her, pull over behind her and come to her rescue, as Sara had just revealed to her. Margo had been lying and sitting on a small cot since her arrival on the craft. Sara and her crew had cleaned her up, tended her wounds and injuries and dressed her in new clean clothes.

"Come on let's get you up," suggested Sara as she helped Margo up onto her feet. Margo found she now was dressed in a one piece silky and shinny outfit to look like Sara and the other ladies on board the spacecraft.

"There are no men on board," observed Margo as she looked around while Sara gave her the tour. The craft was ultra-sleek, quick and silent, and Margo was quite impressed.

"Oh this is the ladies-day cruise special," smiled Sara, "we did not allow men on board this trip."

"Oh," Margo wasn't sure if she should laugh or not. She wasn't sure if Sara was kidding or being serious.

"If we do allow men on board, we hire them to do our bidding and they do not get paid as much as the women do," smiled Sara. "Oh yes, the worm as turned, as the earthlings say."

"Wow, paybacks are hell, as they should be," Margo was glad to hear due justice was in progress somewhere, even if it wasn't on Earth, yet. But Margo felt that times were already changing as more and more women gain in financial status that women will break through all those glass ceilings that white men had so selfishly put up. It was a fact that women made up more than fifty percent of the population, yet only a few where in Congress. More and more democratic women were beginning to run on every political level, local and federal, now. Women were no longer willing to sit idly by and tolerate inequality. Most women had finally come to believe that males are not any wiser or smarter than they were.

Margo was beginning to believe that women were indeed from Venus, the planet of love, and men are from Mars, the aggressive, warlike energy planet. Women demanded equality for they have seen and experienced enough suppression. No longer were people living in the days of totally man-of-the-house breadwinner economics. Not since the 1960s *Ozzie and Harriet* perfect family television show days, which were meant to manipulate and mind control people into perfect gender roll family members. Things were indeed changing, and women were no longer falling in line as second class domestic servants. Women were entering into male orientated professions such as dentists, lawyers, doctors, scientists, enlisted soldiers and much more.

There are more women than men in the country according to the most recent government census. So it only made sense to them to be represented in government positions. And in more recent years, it was evident that more women attended and completed college than men. More and more women were heads of small and medium size businesses. Women were now in every profession, even in the military and outside labor forces that were once solely dominated by men. Margo pondered all these thoughts as the all-female crew showed her around the craft.

Margo enjoyed her tour of the saucer. She was amazed at the futuristic design and operations of the craft. It truly was a craft above all crafts. In that moment Margo was very happy to be a hybrid from Alcyone, the brightest and largest star of the Pleiades star cluster. She was appreciative and honored to have been rescued by Sara and to learn more about herself and her Pleiades origin.

"Come, sit at the controls," offered Sara, "we will help you learn to fly the craft."

"I can't believe that you are going to allow me to fly this craft," Margo stated in astonished wonder, "hope I do okay."

"It's easy, besides, I have faith in you! You just rescued yourself from a submerged vehicle," smiled Sara. She had lots of confidence in Margo's capabilities.

"Easy, it doesn't appear to be easy," stated Margo said as she looked over the large panel of switches and flashing lights.

"You'll see, it's easy," encouraged Sara.

"It looks so complicated." Margo considered herself a quick learner. Every job she had in the past wasn't much of a challenge to her, and she loved being challenged. When she worked for a utility company, she caught on very quickly about the ohms and voltage standards she had to learn, same when she had the learn the ins and outs of the insurance business when she worked in that industry, and now after studying and learning to be a real estate agent, she worked very diligently. She proved her selling skills by winning bonuses for selling the most expensive homes and businesses in the area and getting higher commissions. She was tops in her field and she had received awards to prove it. But still she wondered if she could master the super advanced technology of this marvelous craft. Margo found that Sara was very supportive and reassuring, so she began to relax.

"It's only as complicated as your mind allows it to be," suggested Sara, "Not to worry, all those switches and lights are mostly there for show anyway."

Really, Margo wondered.

"Really, they are not necessary," Sara said with a grin and a twinkle in her big green eyes.

Margo wondered if using switches would be more comfortable than having to concentrate hard enough to fly this so-called craft above all crafts."

"It's easy," insisted Sara, "just direct your thoughts, concentrate and think that you want to head to Alcyone. You'll see it, it's the brightest star of the Pleiades constellation, and the craft will automatically take you there. It's our home, so it knows the way. Just concentrate on the word Alcyone, and it will take you there. In a way it is just a more advanced, fancy tracking global positioning system. All you need to do is just plug in the destination information not by speaking or typing in the information but by thinking about where you wish to go."

"Sure hope my mind doesn't wander," smiled Margo, "and we land on Venus or Mars or some other place."

"You'll be fine," suggested Sara, "the sophisticated guiding system will question you if you suddenly change your mind."

Margo was most impressed by the intricate technology which appeared to be far more advanced than any earthly corporation or government agency had in their stockpile. Margo happily sat behind the controls but was curious as to why they were going to Alcyone, but she kept thinking about the place and the word as the craft swiftly maneuvered through space.

"Why Alcyone?" asked Margo. Having been born on earth she was not aware that she was originally from Alcyone the brightest star of the eight star cluster that made up Pleiades.

"We want to show you where you were from before you decided to reincarnate as a human hybrid on planet Earth. You volunteered to help improve all the negative conditions on Earth and to help prepare humanity's move into the next dimension, the Fifth Dimension of the Age of Aquarius. Hopefully humans will finally evolve and wise up to learn that we are all enlightened souls and part of the universal collective consciousness, and that is what the Fifth Dimension is all about, rising up to a higher consciousness," explained Sara.

"Alcyone, Alcyone, go to Alcyone," sighed Margo, nervously concentrating and mentally repeated over and over again the word "Alcyone." She tried not to think about how excited she was to fly the craft or to see Alcyone. She had to put those thoughts aside as she continued to concentrate on the word, Alcyone , her destiny. She was just a little doubtful of her flying abilities. She thought hard about Alcyone as the craft moved swiftly. Margo was so excited to be behind the controls as the craft maneuvered about the universe in a smooth flow of twists and turns. They passed the Moon, Mars, Venus, and made way further into the Milky Way Galaxy. They passed Orion's Belt. When they got close to Venus in the Constellation of Taurus, Margo spotted the bright star of Alcyone. It felt magical! She marveled at the beauty of space and how the craft was delightfully, nimble, and silent as it maneuvered around the planets and stars. Within minutes they reached their destination and the craft gently landed.

"See, easy," said Sara watching Margo's face light up with the fresh smile of accomplishment.

"Oh, wow, why don't the humans on Earth have this capability, Sara?" asked Margo, "it's so fantastic."

"They do, they received the technology way back in July of 1947 in the Roswell crash. That is why the flying saucer crashed. It crashed in order to leave human beings on earth some advanced technology and materials to reverse engineer. The Pleiadians felt that human beings were too far behind every other planet in the universe, as Earthlings hung on to the old ways of technology for monetary reasons. A handful of rich white men were highly invested in petroleum and wanted to keep it that way even though they knew refineries spewed out toxins into the atmosphere that harmed all life and the environment," said Sara.

"Yes, I can see that corporate heads wanted to hang on to what was working for them at the time and enhancing their profit margins," agreed Margo. "It so sad they were not more concerned about preserving life and the planet."

"Believe it or not, at the turn of the century, around 1905 there were electric cars, they were lighted, silent, clean, and non-polluting. People loved them. But the oil men drove electric car companies out of business so they could promote gasoline cars. They destroyed city electric streetcar rail lines. Los Angeles had hundreds of miles of electric streetcar rail lines which they could surely use now. But the auto industry and oil men spoke, and bought up and yanked all the streetcar rails which were replaced with miles and miles of roadways. Only to be accentuated by the Eisenhower Interstate roadways project after WWII when city dwellers were marrying and moving to the suburbs. Planned communities sprung up and swallowed up acres of prime planting soil. Young couples moved to the new post-war prefab manufactured Levittown suburb homes to raise families. Oil men knew refineries spread tons and tons of toxic pollution in the air, but did not care, that was just the cost of doing business, just like collateral damage was a fact of their wars. Big business only cared about the bottom line of their selfish profits. They say it was all for the shareholders, but they made sure that the head executives got their bonuses right off the top before shareholders saw any returns. The elitist Anunnaki Reptilian greedy ones hung onto the old ways because that is where the wealthy had their money invested. These elitist cared nothing about future technology of less earth-damaging resources water, wind, and solar power. These greedy heads of wealthy corporations and large campaign contributors of conservatives wanted to keep their profits invested in oil until the last drop of oil came out of the ground and was refined and sold for profit.

The American greedy are very obstinate, arrogant Anunnaki Reptilian descendants who knew, but did not care, that they were ruining the planet. And others were too naive to see what they were doing, and felt powerless, or did not care. People were lied to because the corporations that controlled the government by way of campaign funds, wanted to keep the real reasons for using petroleum secret, big profits for a few. The church, advertising firms, and the media help with propaganda to control the masses, separating and corralling them into neatly-tailored gender social rolls.

Chapter Ten

Margo remembered when she was a kid and heard her mother say that all girls wanted the same thing and that was to be married and have babies. Newly married couples wanted to have a boy first in order to carry on the family name and business. Girls were to help mom with cooking, cleaning and the younger siblings. It's what Margo's mother told her. Margo dreaded her pre-programmed short list itinerary of her future. To Margo's dismay nothing was ever said about love--there were no hugs, only work.

Back in the fifties, mothers were told not to spoil their babies. That it was good to let the baby cry, in order to toughen them up. Boys were spoiled and allowed to be mean to smaller boys and girls. Margo knew that firsthand, as she had the knots on her head and the bruises on her arms to show for it. Her brother was a tyrant. The idea was that boys needed to be toughened up in order to fight wars. Margo wondered, *must there be wars, can't people talk things out? Perhaps if you did not raise boys to be mean bullies they would not grow up to be mean, angry, selfish, autocrats who only know to divide, conquer and enslave.*

Margo thought that most wars were initiated not for enabling democracy in countries as they say, but rather are capitalist driven corporate leaders influencing generals to find reasons to attack third world countries in order to gain power over their land, oil, minerals and domination over the people.

It bothered Margo to think that greedy corporate heads thought that they were gods and that planet Earth was to be used fully to serve themselves. They did not care about the planet itself nor the life forms that inhabited it, it was more of a competitive sport amongst the males so it seemed to Margo.

"Greed puts Earth way behind all the other planetary civilizations of the universe who are using solar and wind and magnetic power which is readily available to everyone," Sara told Margo.

Margo knew that back at the turn of the twentieth century, an inventor named Nikola Tesla, per Sara, a Pleiadian hybrid, had it right. He had it figured out. He had developed wireless electrical transmission between distance electrical towers that were grounded to the earth's magnetic force; thus providing free electricity for all, wirelessly. It was free electricity without wires to be used as free energy for all. But a couple of rich businessmen competed, and those two men needed money, and a greedy banker who owned copper mines agreed to help out monetarily, but he wanted to run electricity over copper wires; so it became the law of the land.

"Wealth and self-serving greed caused the inhabitants of Earth to be forced to remain very far behind the rest of the universe which was much more advanced technologically. It is why your earth governments hide the fact that we Pleiadians and other extraterrestrials exist. It's all about Annunaki Reptilian Aryan white extremists and their control and their power over the whole population of the Earth, and beyond, if they could," said Sara.

Margo had no idea why those men would want to do that. Why? Margo was sad about the fact that men remain so barbaric out of greed for themselves and not for the welfare of humanity. And to Margo, that proved that human males are descendants from the Fourth Dimension Anunnaki Reptilian Martian line created to be earthling slaves. This is easily seen as men fall behind the loudest, demanding leader who commands over them. These men make loyal soldiers who do not question authority.

"So, we are going to fix all of that, right?" asked Margo feeling vulnerable herself but allowing a slight sense of hope to slip into her otherwise dreadful sad feelings of the way things were for women on the planet. She could not see how she could help just being one person, and a woman at that. Margo was beginning to see the big picture though. Men were unwilling to help women and children better their lives, so the Pleiadians secretly stepped in. Pleiadians were the watchers, the overseers of planet Earth and their job was to protect Earth from destruction.

"Yes," sighed Sara, "we will try to help the women and children of earth rise up to be equal to the male status, in fact, we may even reverse situations a bit. This Fourth Dimension Anunnaki Reptilian mentality has caused great havoc on Earth, but you and I and others like us are here to usher in the Fifth Dimension age of Aquarius feminine ruled by we Pleiadians," warned Sara.

"It's that serious isn't it," realized Margo, "and my husband being no better than the rest of the delinquents on Earth."

"Because they are delinquents, we are forced to interfere in our subtle ways," explained Sara. She went on to explain further. "Of course, we must follow Galactic rule and not show our forces or reveal our sources. However, in times of unclear war threat, and the building of the Atom bomb near the end of Earth's World War II it was important to display deterrents. To show our disappointment and disapproval, we have flown several spacecrafts over Washington at various times to show our distaste and our strength.

"In all troubling times when humans do not use their common sense by safeguarding the sanctity of life we had to show our might. The Anunnaki Reptilians are back at it again as hybrid humans. Especially the male population, are very stubborn, power hungry, and only see dollar signs in their eyes," warned Sara.

"Margo that is why there are Pleiadian hybrids

born on planet Earth to help circulate mental powers of change throughout the population, as I have said, according to galactic rule, we are not supposed to interfere. But egotistical narcissistic corporate leaders do not yield. Things have gotten so bad on Earth that they are ruining the planet, and we feel we must intervene once again. The balance in social power to energy between male and female realities needed to be adjusted. The Pleiadians were trying to protect planet Earth. Because if planet Earth is rendered uninhabitable and if the human experiment fails, then that negative collective cosmic energy will throw off the balance of the whole Milky Way galactic system, and we cannot allow that to happen," explained Sara.

"It is so horrible," expressed Margo, "and has gone on for far too long. Is it getting worse?"

She had much more to say so continued as Margo sat quietly and listened intently to Sara's every word. "It's not all their fault, for we are all star seeds. But many men are descendants of Anunnaki Reptilian races. And they come from the more aggressive war mongering planet of Mars. And most women are from the more loving, kinder, balanced planet of Venus. Notice how the rich men want to go to Mars and build colonies in which to live?"

She thought perhaps subconsciously even if not knowing why, like trained homing pigeons, conservative men want to return back to their own home planet of Mars. Margo also noticed how nothing was ever mentioned about the planet Venus by men. She thought of course, *it's because the men who make themselves the rulers are self-centered and make it all about their wants and needs and deny everyone else. With no balance between the two energies, the evil ones from Mars rose up to dominate. There needs to be an enhanced Mars-Venus balance which has always been drastically off balance. But there is hope.*

Chapter Eleven

"You did an excellent job flying the craft, my dear," declared Sara regarding Margo's flying capabilities and superb landing skills. Margo was almost overcome with excitement when she saw the beautiful Alcyone landscape with its lush green valleys, majestic mountains, giant oak trees, ultra-modern land, and space-capsules soaring around tall, cloud-reaching sleek futuristic buildings and small personal space-capsules docked adjacent to apartment patios. Margo had never seen a more futuristic city. It gave her hope for America and beyond. She saw firsthand what was possible. Sara was only too happy to show Margo all around Alcyone.

"Oh, it is so beautiful here," exclaimed Margo as she stood and turned slowly in a circle taking in the beauty of Alcyone. In ways it was much like the forest on Earth, only the oak trees where very tall, reaching high up into the skies. Margo was very impressed by the anti-gravity silent solar-powered space capsule vehicles that glided high up off the ground and around and about the ultra-space-scraper solar-powered buildings with sonic and global tracking guiding systems that kept them from colliding with buildings and other vehicles.

"I love the sleek design of the tall twisting spiral glass buildings that rise up toward the universe through wispy white clouds. It's so futuristic! Cities on earth looked old fashioned and antiquated in comparison. Unlike polluted conditions on planet Earth, the Pleiades and the central star Alcyone atmosphere was crystal clear, air, soil, water, food is all fresh, organic, grown without any chemicals. It was very plain to Margo after Sara explained that Earth was a learning and self-testing planet where most, but not all humans, succeed. Negative energy persists as they try but somehow fail to learn and progress.

"Yes, we are very proud of Alcyone," Sara admitted. "Come let me show you my living quarters."

The occupants departed the sleek silver saucer and boarded a commuter sized space-capsule that silently floated through the aerial highways and by-ways of the magical futuristic style city. The sleek capsule glided around the tall sleek buildings and in minutes arrived at Sara's living quarters. Her floor to ceiling windowed, one story apartment unit was in one of those super tall sleek buildings they circled. Sara brought the capsule gently to a halt and latched it onto the parking bracket attached to the spacious patio of the apartment. Margo looked around and there was various styled craft latched onto balconies just as Sara parked hers. Sara and Margo stepped out of the craft, onto her patio and into Sara's apartment.

"This is so beautiful," admired Margo. She could tell Sara felt very proud of Alcyone. The futuristic designed apartment with its many lovely features was nearly all white, very sleek and efficient with a full display of feminine decorating features. There were various plants, multi-colored accent pieces of art and beautiful wide-plank oak wood floors, ceiling to floor windows and accented brick walls. Margo immediately felt at home.

"Is that oak?" asked Margo.

"Yes," answered Sara.

"I love the wide plank oak wood floors," complimented Margo.

"Yes, all the wood is from the large forest of oak trees throughout Alcyone," Sara pointed out.

"It is very lovely here," Margo marveled at the idea that each apartment had a small glass greenhouse area where residence could grow their own vegetables and fruits. Everything they ate was fresh out of the garden and off the vine. The sky was so beautifully clear and the air so fresh and clean.

"I want to stay here, Earth is so barbaric and backwards especially with all the fighting and greed that is so obvious in corporations and governments. Can I stay here until Earth is fully into the Fifth Dimension and all of the Anunnaki Reptilian negative energies are gone?" sighed Margo.

"I understand your concerns, my dear," Sara smiled. "We are fortunate to be so free here on Alcyone. Females on Alcyone are very much Aquarian and therefore androgynous and can either mate with a male or another female or impregnate themselves, via the science of harvesting stem cells from their own bone marrow, the choice is theirs. They choose. Our males here are very attractive, and unlike males on Earth, are not egotistical and authoritarian. There is no hate. Everyone loves each other and gets along for the greater good of all. You on Earth see an act of kindness and it makes you cry, because you feel it is so rare. Well, there would be no need for those tears here, not here on Alcyone or anywhere in the Pleiades, we are a nation of pure love. There is a monetary system but inhabitants also barter and trade goods and services. Our space- capsules, like that we rode here in are driven by magnetic quantum crystal power, the same as our spacecrafts. It is clean energy. Everyone here is healthy, our food is authentic and organic. The corporate and political systems in your country unfortunately do not appear to care if they make people sick, as it only adds to their profits. On Alcyone we use a type of currency. We have several over-sight agencies keeping an eye on each other and beyond. We are governed by our own shared universal consciousness. We are fair and loving. We just do not have the narcissistic greed and hate that people on Earth have," explained Sara.

"It's so amazing here." Margo wanted to stay.

"I can certainly understand that you want to stay here on Alcyone and not go back to Earth. But I must remind you that you chose to be birthed on Earth as a Pleiadian hybrid and therefore you should make an attempt to finish out your assignment if at all possible. I will help. We do not usually interfere, but in some cases, we feel it is necessary to protect our many hybrids born on primitive planet Earth. Of course you do not remember that you chose to be born a volunteer Pleiadian hybrid on planet Earth, that's half the fun of the adventure," Sara said with a smile.

"Are you sure I cannot abandon my mission and stay here with you?" asked Margo with a longing in her voice she could not hide.

"Sorry, my dear," sighed Sara, "but, I will only be a thought away. So just think of me, call my name and I'll be there." Sara went on to further explain to Margo the journey she chose to undertake:

"To prove that you are one of us, you are of a single cell Pleiadian DNA, and have no desire for body art, you are loving and kind and are attracted to love people with emotional problems. You are a soul healer because you understand the ability to feel the soul and its loving energy. And therefore, in your hybrid localities, you might remain in an unhappy relationship for many years, or have a hard time understanding why your partner has left you after you worked three jobs to help pay his way through medical school. That should explain why you married Jack. You are loyal, loving and want to help," explained Sara hoping this explanation would help Margo understand her mission on earth.

"Well, I will not mind being a Pleiadian hybrid on planet Earth, if it helps improve people's attitudes to move forward in the right direction in order to save the planet," explained Margo.

"Come we must go, it's time to get you back to planet Earth," smiled Sara leading Margo back out onto the shuttle capsule vehicle.

"I really do not want to return to Earth," sighed Margo taking a longing look around at the beautiful peaceful, well organized city base.

"You must for just a little while longer," promised Sara.

"So, I have to die on planet Earth before I can return here to Alcyone ?"

"Not necessarily, we'll see what we can do," promised Sara.

"That is certainly good to know. Thanks Sara for rescuing me and taking good care of me."

"Of course, my dear," smiled Sara

"I will miss this place and you," Margo said sounding sad.

"We will continue looking over you," Sara said as she nudged Margo a bit to get her moving.

"Come it's time to fly, you drive," laughed Sara giving Margo a quick hug before leading her into the craft.

Margo was all smiles; she loved to fly the craft. "Where are we going next?" Margo asked wishing to take a detour before heading back to Earth.

"It is time for you to go back to the house, " Sara informed Margo and then watched her frown. The only thing that made it better was that she got to fly the saucer, and Sara promised she would see her again very soon.

Chapter Twelve

As if waking up from what felt like an extraordinary exciting and a little scary dream, Margo found herself in her own house, lying on her own couch. She looked around in awe and wondered, *did it really happen? Did the accident, the driver, her husband, running her off the road, meeting Sara.* She wondered, *did all that really happen? And if it really did happen, why was she back in her house?* She wasn't sure how long she was gone, it felt like days. She thought back and figured it had to be more than six days. But it really did happen. All Margo had to do was look down at the clothes she wore now; the silver soft smooth material of the all-in-one pants suit outfit that she wore. So yes, it did truly happen. Suddenly she missed Sara, and beautiful Alcyone. Margo had been with Sara for what seems like several earth-days but she couldn't tell for sure because on Alcyone there is no time as we track it on earth.

Margo felt sad. Why wasn't she still with Sara in the magnificent silver saucer. And then she remembered the accident with the car in the flooded waters and became frightened at the memory. She did not belong there in this house any longer; it made her feel very uneasy.

Margo began looking around at her surroundings, she got up from the couch and looked out the window and indeed saw that her car was gone. The only thing Margo saw in the driveway were several daily delivered newspapers. She knew her car would not be found until all the flood water had subsided; and with all the rain lately, *that could take weeks*, she thought. *Where was Jack anyway?* Margo wondered. His truck was gone. Margo, had no idea what she would do next. She decided that for now she would just lay low.

Where was Jack? He had turned her life upside down. Margo remembered that she was smitten by Jack when they met. She fell hard and fast and was eager to be married to him when he proposed shortly after they met. She knew it was fast, but she was madly in love. But it wasn't long before the honeymoon was over. Some months after they were married, Margo began to see a darker side to Jack that was hidden behind the handsome flirtatious facade he presented to her and the public . They argued more, he ridiculed her on a daily basis as if she couldn't do anything right. She had decided to divorce him. She was about to serve him divorce papers. Why should she suffer emotional trauma, after all she had a great job as a real estate agent; she was one of the top sellers in her area. And she was keeping most of the money she made and investing it for her retirement. She really didn't need Jack at all, especially now that he had shown his cruel angry side. She hated the thought of going through a contested divorce. She wished she could have stayed with Sara on Alcyone.

Margo wondered, why, if Sara saved her and took her up to the spacecraft, why didn't she keep her there in the craft, or at Alcyone; just anywhere besides sending her back to this house where Jack would be returning. Margo couldn't make any sense of it. She wondered what she had missed while she was gone. So she decided to run out and get the newspapers she saw in the driveway and see what day it was.

Margo hurried out the front door and down the front porch steps onto the driveway and quickly retrieved the wrapped newspapers and rushed back inside. She did not want any of the neighbors to see her. It was bad enough she did not know where Jack was nor when he would be returning. Her plan was to be packed and out of there before he returned. She quickly unfolded newspapers and began reading the headlines.

The headline on the oldest dated newspaper caught her eye, it was about a woman who was reported missing recently. Her co-workers were looking for her. She left no contact information of next of kin. Finally, it was decided that she was thought to have run off with a truck driver who was a regular customer at the diner. Co-workers in the diner said he no longer showed up at the diner either. They said he used to sit at the counter and chat with the woman who was now missing. When questioned, co-workers figured she just left town with him. But expressed their thoughts that she did not seem like the type to not tell the boss of her plans. Margo hoped that the woman was all right.

She proceeded to open and read the most recent newspaper and almost fainted. When Margo opened the most recently dated newspaper her attention was quickly drawn to her own name.

"What!" she said out loud to herself, feeling lightheaded and suddenly sick to her stomach. The article reported that she had died when her car ran off rain slick roads down into flooded waters. She searched on for more information and that was when she saw further down in the article, her own funeral arrangements; *nothing like reading your own obituary* she thought. The article in the newspaper reported that she, Margo Jones, beloved wife of Jack Jones died in an auto accident in flooded water. She was angry. He could have at least said that she was an award-winning real estate agent. She went on to read the article which included her funeral arrangement information. The funeral was this very day. Margo felt as if she were in shock, and could not believe what she had just been through, the accident, the saucer and the trip to Alcyone. But now she had to decide what she was going to do about facing her own death, her own funeral was this very day. But she was alive sitting in her own living room on the sofa reading her own obituary. She wondered, if I am here, just who is in my coffin being buried in my place? Then suddenly she felt a rock of reality punch her in the gut... was it the missing waitress?

Chapter Thirteen

Margo assumed that Jack needed a body for the funeral in order to claim the insurance money. Margo only had to wonder for a moment, because it did not take Margo long to put two and two together. Did Jack kill that woman so he would have a body? Margo imagined that Jack had probably the shock of his life when he went back to the scene of the crime and found her partially submerged car, but not her. She thought Jack probably assumed her body drifted out of the car into the flood waters and that some animals got to it.

Margo's intuition told her that her husband, Jack, was involved with the other woman's disappearance. It was plain to Margo that he needed a body to prove her death to the insurance company. It was very clear to Margo that Jack was determined not to waste any time in getting her buried and getting the life insurance policy money.

Well it should be a small funeral since my parents are deceased and she had no family left. She figured though that her co-workers and her friend Claire would attend. Margo felt like crying. She felt sorry for her friend Claire, she wanted to call her and tell that that it was all a terrible mistake, that she was indeed still alive. She also thought about dressing in a disguise and attending her own funeral, but that plan was spoiled when she looked at the clock and saw that it was too late and services would have been over by now.

As she sat quietly in her living-room she began to worry. *What if he comes back home to the house to get something, or has invited people to come over to the house after the funeral services?* Suddenly Margo's heart jumped as she saw a car pull into the driveway. To her amazement and hurtful heart, it was her friend, Joe. Joe was her husband, Jack's, cousin. When Margo first began dating Jack, she met his cousin Joe and they immediately clicked and easily became friends. Margo did not know what to do now as he was heading for the house. She was in a panic. She was about to jump up and slip out the backdoor when she saw the front door handle turn and the door slowly open.

"Oh crap," Margo said in a frightened whispered. She had no time to even turn and run as Joe slowly opened the door and stepped into the front foyer in plain view of where she sat. He stood for a moment as if letting his eyes adjust to the dimness of the room. After a minute he slowly looked around as if sensing that someone was there in the room with him. Margo was too frozen with fright to even try to speak.

"Holy shit," Joe whispered as if he couldn't believe

his eyes. Was he seeing who he thought he was seeing? Was he going mad? He had just attended her funeral. As he entered the living-room he strained his eyes to get a better look at who was sitting there on the sofa. The closer he got to Margo the bigger his eyes grew and the whiter his face. Joe could barely catch his breath.

"Take it easy," Margo pleaded. "Yes, it's me," she warned in a low voice. To herself she thought she sounded apologetic, as if she felt guilty for being alive and scaring him. It was all the strength that Margo could muster to talk in a voice just barely above a whisper. She couldn't move, the torturous look on Joe's face made her feel odd, foreign, dead, alien, other worldly. She watched as Joe flopped himself down in a chair. He looked faint and very pale as if he was seeing a ghost.

"Holy crap," Joe said with wide eyes and a pale face.

"Yes, it's me, all right," smiled Margo, "I'm alive."

"Am I going nuts?" he blurted out, "what the ... "

"No, you are not going nuts," Margo advised quickly, afraid Joe was about to go berserk. She got up and walked closer to Joe. She sat down in a chair opposite from him. She was disturbed and disgusted that they even had to have this conversation because of her idiot husband.

"I just came from your freaking funeral. I went to the cemetery and saw you buried," Joe spoke as if he couldn't catch his breath. He was practically hysterical between tears and laughter as he rushed over to Margo to touch her to make sure that he was really seeing his friend. Margo just looked at him strangely wishing none of this was happening.

"It's all okay, really," assured Margo, "it is what it is." She was in shock too and she knew it.

"But, if you were not buried, then who was buried?" Joe asked in a frantic voice. Suddenly realizing he had witnessed something very wrong at Margo's funeral.

"I don't know, maybe you should ask your cousin and my near husband, the widower Jack, what's going on," suggested Margo in an almost too casual tone for the bazaar situation she found herself in. She may have sounded casual, but she knew she had the look of dread. It was so like Jack to pull something like this. Just goes to show how love is blind and how we never bother to connect the dots or collect the history on our potential lovers and life mates. Suddenly Margo wished she would have had her friend Claire's brother, a state patrolman, do a criminal check on Jack when she met him. But, who thinks of that when you meet a very nice good looking guy. *It's such a rare find anyway these days,* Margo thought. *When you meet a nice guy it is easy to believe what you want to believe, and totally forget about the old saying, "if it seems too good to be true, it usually is."*

"Oh, things are beginning to make sense now," sighed Joe, "anyway, I think they are. I just need to stay sitting down for a minute or two more. This is getting to be too much."

"What do you mean," asked Margo, "that things are beginning to make sense now?"

"Well, I wish now I would have said something earlier but hindsight is twenty-twenty they say. Jack has been widowed before he met you, actually twice."

"Oh, I see," Margo was beginning to feel foolish, like another unsuspecting love fool. Silently, mentally she scolded herself. She should had known better.

Margo was upset. So that was how Jack made his money, through marrying unsuspecting lonely women then helping them meet their demise and collecting life insurance policy money he had on them; that is, I guess unless he could get a hold of a rich woman. Margo's shock was turning into pure unadulterated anger. She did not like the idea of being fooled or being the victim. Her anger gave her strength for thoughts of retaliation. But first she thought she better take care of Joe who looked dreadfully pale. She quickly stepped into the kitchen and retrieved a bottle of water from the refrigerator.

"Joe, here drink some water," demanded Margo as she handed him a cold bottle of water, "you look pale, like you are about to faint."

"I feel like I am about to faint," Joe replied in a low voice taking the water and leaning back in the chair. He thanked her and held the cold bottle to this forehead for a moment before taking a big drink. Immediately he felt much better.

"Whew," Joe whispered as he couldn't catch his breath, his heart was beating so fast and his head felt light and dizzy. The cold bottle against his head made him feel better.

"I am so sorry that I shocked you." Margo felt bad for him.

"I cried at your funeral, you know," confessed Joe still trying to catch his breath. "You know not many people can make such a statement," he added suddenly realizing the gravity of what he had just said. He burst into a sharp painful sound of forced laughter.

"No shit," responded Margo feeling strangely lightheaded then uncapped the bottle of water she held in her hand and took a much needed big gulp.

"This is awful," said Joe. "Just what has Jack done?" This time, he added under his breath.

"Oh, my, I feel like fainting," repeated Joe ever so faintly has he slouched into the cushions. He knew all of this was not going to end well for Jack. Joe just realized Jack committed at least three crimes, attempted man slaughter, insurance fraud, and kidnapping and murder of the waitress. Since the waitress was missing, Joe and Margo could only assume that she was the one used to replace Margo in order to collect the life insurance money.

"Hey, I'm supposed to be the one who feels like fainting," Margo remarked angrily going to the kitchen to get another bottle of water for her and Joe. She handed Joe a new bottle of water then flopped down on the sofa across from him and quickly opened the bottle and took a long drink. "After all, my husband has just buried me."

They were both pale and looked like they were about to faint. Joe slowly removed his tie and unbuttoned his shirt collar . He took a deep breath, sat back and drank half the bottle in one gulp. In a few minutes, Margo noticed that his color was returning and she told him so. They both were beginning to feel better.

"Sorry, but I did feel like I was about to pass out, the water really helped," Joe said in a soft voice leaning back into the sofa. Joe was Jack's cousin but was like a brother to Margo.

"Here drink more water," insisted Margo getting up to get two more bottles from the refrigerator and placing another bottle of water on the coffee table in front of him.

"Thanks," said her friend in a weak voice as he uncapped the bottled water and took a long drink. It was cold and felt good going down his dry parched throat.

"So, do you get the picture of what is going on here?" asked Margo.

"Yes, I do believe I do," Joe cleared his throat and got up then from the chair and went over to the sofa to sit next to Margo where he gave her a long hug.

"Damn, I thought you were dead. I have been crying ever since I heard about the accident. So guess that missing waitress I read about in the newspaper got buried in your place." Joe stated.

"It appears so," said Margo, "I wondered what poor soul took my place."

"I can't believe Jack could do such horrible things," explained Joe then took another drink of water. Jack and I pretty much grew up together, but through the years, he has worked and lived in various places throughout the country so we sort of lost track of each other. But, I still can't believe he would do such a horrible thing.

"You never know about anyone, really, do we?" stated Margo she still felt as if she were in shock. First, the crash, trapped and fighting to get out of the submerged car, then the spacecraft experience, then discovering that it was her very own husband who tried to kill her, and then discover that he killed someone else to bury in her place. She wondered just how much can a gal take at one time? She began shaking.

"You're shaking," stated Joe and he began searching his jacket pocket until he found the small vile of pills that he was searching for.

"I do feel pretty stressed," Margo said in a soft voice as she sat back on the couch. She had been through a lot already and now this.

"Here take this Valium, it'll help calm you down," Joe held out his hand with the tiny white pill laying in his open palm. Usually she didn't take any medication for fear of it being habitual and having side effects. But, in this case without thinking much about it, she grabbed the tiny pill in her left hand, put it in her mouth immediately following with her right hand, took a long drink from the bottled water. Margo did not think much about it, she just wanted to escape the whole situation. She was very ready to calm down. She let out a sigh. It was difficult to face the fact that the person you love, lived, and slept with every night tried to kill you. And in a way he did kill her, because now she was ostracized from her job, her friends, who now thought she was dead and buried. Only one thing good came of it. She met Sara.

It was only by the grace of her spiritual guides and her Pleiadian soul sister Sara, that she was indeed still living and breathing on this Earth. She sat for a few minutes with her eyes closed as Joe got up and sat in the recliner. He sat there and watched her to make sure the Valium would help and she would relax. He was surprised when in a few minutes Margo opened her eyes and asked him a question.

"You read the article in the paper where that woman went missing recently," Margo asked.

"Yes, I did," Joe said, "what are you saying, that Jack could not find your body at the wreckage so got another body?"

"Let's think of the possibility that when Jack did not find my body in or near the wrecked car that he panicked and merely went about to find another body to bury so he could claim the life insurance money," Margo could not believe her own thoughts and words. Who would do such a thing? The thought made her realize she did not know Jack at all. He always was a little mysterious, never really sharing any stories about his childhood or his past. He told her he was heavy into stock and bond trading and that was how he made all of his money. He was so kind and generous at the beginning, that she believed him.

"How can that be," asked Joe, "it's so unbelievable."

"And I guess our law enforcement agency, the coroner and the morgue felt no reason to do any physical testing to identify the body as Jack identified the body as being his wife. They had no reason to doubt him." Margo was becoming aware of many factors that possibly contributed to the situation she was in now.

"Jack cried at your funeral," stated Joe, "I saw him cry."

"Is that supposed to make me feel better?" Margo wanted to know. Then she decided Joe did not mean that in a vicious manner. Before he could say anything in his defense, Margo spoke again.

"Well, we'll add 'actor' then to his repertoire of many secret talents," Margo said sarcastically.

"So, Jack forced you off the road," Joe was astonished, "and when he went back and could not find your body in the car, he just went out and got another one. I can't believe it. Jack has gone totally mad then."

"So it appears." Margo agreed. "The newspaper article said the woman was a transient person, someone who was fairly new in town who worked nights as a waitress at a local diner. She only worked there for a very short time before she did not report to work and came up missing leaving some of her things and her car behind. The other waitresses at the diner said they saw her being friendly to a tall middle-aged guy who regularly came into the diner later in the evening when she was working. Someone said that he was a truck driver. The reporter who wrote the piece said the woman had not worked there very long. So when she failed to show up for her shift three nights in a row and they never heard from her, they just figured she decided to leave town, probably with the same man since they never saw him again either. They did not find anything helpful in her locker at work, only a jacket, pockets were empty, there was nothing with a phone number. She wasn't even there long enough to receive her fist bi- weekly paycheck. They thought maybe she went off with the long distance truck driver because neither of them were seen again at the diner," read Margo.

"Interesting," said Joe half listening and then appearing distracted as he looked Margo up and down. *What a curious outfit,* he thought. He had been wondering and finally his curiosity got the better of him.

"What are you looking at," wondered Margo, when she suddenly remembered the ladies in the spacecraft and the outfit they dressed her in. Why didn't she think to change cloths. But the one-piece jumpsuit style outfit was so comfortable she did not even think about changing into something else.

"I've been meaning to ask, is that casual wear or night clothes that you are wearing," Joe wondered, "looks very comfortable."

"Yes, it is very comfortable, do you like it?" asked Margo with a smile, and suddenly feeling a little nervous that Joe's curiosity may get the better of him.

"Yes, I do like it. The fabric looks beautiful, comfy and a bit unusual, one might say, other worldly," Joe answered. He had to admit he had never seen such fabric before. He had to feel it. He couldn't resist and wanted to see it closer. So he got up from the couch and took a few steps closer to get a better look. He had to touch it, and lightly rubbed the fabric of her sleeve between his index finger and thumb.

"Oh it's very fine fabric, indeed, although a bit unusual, I must say. I sew some, and have never seen this type of material in any fabric stores," Joe said. Joe always wanted to be s seamstress and design men and women's casual clothing. He tried, but found the job opportunities were limited and he did not have the startup capital to begin his own business venture. So reluctantly he ditched the designer dream and settled for a career working as an insurance broker. Still through the years, he was determined to fulfill his dream, so as soon as he saved enough money he planned to start up his own business designing casual comfort clothes. He had to touch the fabric again. He loved the fabric. He was looking Margo over from head to toe.

"Yes, it is very unusual isn't it. It is made out of a fabric that you cannot find anywhere around here," Margo said, and she knew that for a fact. Joe continued looking Margo up and down. He was feeling much better now. The fainting sensations and nausea feelings had subsided. He leaned way back to take another long look at Margo. He had her get up from the couch and turn around. He liked the outfit. It looked very attractive on her as it showed off her nice figure and sensuous curves. It felt a little silly, but he just had to tell her what he thought.

"I must say, my dear, death becomes you," Joe giggled almost feeling embarrassed for making a joke out of a dreadful situation. Then thought that sometimes it is better to laugh then to cry. And besides, how many times in your life, if ever, do you get the chance to say those words?

"Why, thank you." Margo began to giggle too. It sounded strange to her; but, she had to admit that the whole situation she found herself in was very bizarre, indeed.

Margo was glad Joe made the comment and they began laughing. She was also glad he did not question her further about the outfit she wore, as she was more worried than flattered. Because, for now, she did not want to reveal any part of her earlier experiences with Sara, her crew or their trip to the Pleiades brightest central star, their home, Alcyone.

She wanted to move on, but for some reason Joe wouldn't let up about her appearance.

"Your hair looks a lighter blond and longer, or is it my imagination?" Joe was amazed at her lovely appearance. Joe had not seen Margo for while, it had been several weeks anyway. At this point it was all beginning to be a little too much for him. He felt in a daze. This whole thing with Jack and Margo was becoming overwhelming. No wonder he felt faint.

"I think you're just glad to see me alive," Margo said and they both laughed again.

"I sure am," sighed Joe.

Margo had to get down to seriousness for she did not do anything different to her hair, well she didn't, but Sara's team did. Margo was not ready to divulge that to Joe, maybe another time. Right now she wanted to change the subject a bit so she asked Joe a question.

"Tell me, did you speak with Jack at the funeral?" she eagerly asked.

"Only to offer my condolences," offered Joe. But right now he was more concerned about what Margo was going to do about Jack faking her death to get the insurance money.

"Can't believe he tried to kill me," offered Margo feeling sad at the thought.

"So are you going to expose him of his fraud and lies?" asked Joe.

"Well, at the moment I have no identification to prove that I am who I am." sighed Margo. "I have been pronounced deceased, remember?"

"Oh, I never thought about that," confessed Joe, "it may be your word against his."

"Yes, how do I prove I am me?" said Margo. She quickly ran to his office desk in the other room. Opened every drawer. She could tell it had been rummaged through. And some files were missing.

"That could be a real problem," Joe said with a serious tone.

"I'm dead," Margo said in a low voice, "I was buried, my very existence was buried along with that's woman's body."

"Well, yes that's true," admitted Joe. "Also, I think if I were you, I would be a little afraid of Jack right about now."

"Why?" wondered Margo.

"If he should ever find out that you are alive," said Joe, "he can't have you alive and revealing his evil ways."

"Tell me about it," stated Margo. And then she hoped that she could trust Joe to not tell Jack that she was still alive.

"You may want to hide out," suggested Joe.

"Joe, I need you to promise not to say anything to Jack, about me being alive, promise?" Margo pleaded in a very serious tone.

"Margo, what are you going to do?" Joe asked. "You can't stay here, he'll be back in a few minutes, I'm sure."

"Joe, I need time to think things through. I need to know for sure if I can trust that you will not mention to anyone that you saw me today. Don't tell anyone until I can come up with a plan. Okay?" Margo said with concern and in all seriousness.

"Sure, no problem," Joe said only too eager to oblige her wishes. "You can count on me." And at the moment he actually meant it. But at the same time his mind was whirling with this knowledge. He wondered how he could use it to his advantage by perhaps blackmailing Jack.

"I am counting on you," replied Margo, "after all, if you expose me, you expose Jack. Are you ready for that big mess to spring up on your account?"

"No, that whole idea makes me feel like fainting again." Joe had to admit but also in the back of his mind he continued to wonder how he could take advantage of this situation. Perhaps, he could blackmail Jack, but for now he quickly put that thought out of his mind and decided he wasn't that kind of guy.

"I need to have a plan," suggested Margo.

"Yes, I agree," offed Joe. "If there is any way I can help, just let me know."

Time was passing and both of them knew that Jack would probably be coming back to the house soon. Joe shifted in his seat as if he was about to get up to leave. He was feeling anxious for himself and for Margo, because he was sure that Jack would be coming back to the house soon.

"But aren't you afraid that he may come back here, to the house, I mean like now, or very soon," warned Joe. "I mean after all, he lives here. And I am sure by now the church luncheon is all over and done with."

"Yes, I am concerned about that. I think that sooner or later, he will come here, so I need to leave, now," admitted Margo. She thought she may stay with Joe at his place or with her real estate agency co-worker and friend, Claire, at her apartment.

"But where will you stay?" asked Joe.

"I was hoping that I could stay with you," confessed Margo.

"Oh, I don't know if that is such a good idea. After Nancy lost her battle with cancer, in my grief, I began knocking out walls to remodel the house. So it's all torn up. It was a great stress release, though. So while it's torn up I will have it remodeled to update the kitchen and bath. And I am planning on creating a sewing and design studio space. Sorry, normally I would say yes, but it's kind of a crazy time right now. "

"Oh, I understand, completely." Margo was sorry to hear that he could not put her up but totally understood under the circumstances. She would think of something else. She decided not to contact Claire, her best friend at work. At the moment she did not want to shock her friend, nor did she want to get her friend involved, not just yet anyway.

"I'm so sorry, but at this point I have no place to actually keep you much less hide you," Joe admitted.

"Well, okay, let me think of something else then," suggested Margo. She was disappointed that her friend Joe could not help her out, but she understood. He would just have to find another place to stay, rather to hide out, until she decided to come forth and expose Jack's wrongful doings.

"What else can I do, how else can I help you?" asked Joe.

"Just do not tell anyone that you saw me," insisted Margo. "I think I have another plan in the works, and I will stay in touch, okay."

"Okay, please do, and I am so sorry, that I could not help" admitted Joe.

Margo was hurt, but she understood. Besides, Sara was just a thought away, all she had to do was think about her Pleiadian friend Sara and Sara would show up in a few minutes and she could discuss the matter with her.

Chapter Fourteen

Joe then left and Margo sat and cried and thought about how she got where she was now. She was not particularly fond of men right now, period. When she spoke in general about men, she had a way of grouping all men together into one negative category until, on an individual basis, they proved themselves otherwise. Sad to think that so far the men in her life since birth were all negative inspirations. Her father was cold and distance and there were no signs of encouragement or loving hugs, no pats on the back for doing good in school, no encouragement to succeed at all. It was as if women were secondary citizens and should be kept down on the lowest rung of the social ladder. Patriarchal rule saw to that. Women did not write the Bible, men wrote the Bible and started up religions of commandments and fear all in the effort to control people; making women, minorities and children total second class citizens ruled by men. And their legal, health and livelihoods were controlled by the males in their lives. Her brother took behavior clues from her father and if he wasn't punching her for grins, he switched his behavior to being nice only for her to soon realize that he just wanted something from her. It hurt her feelings and made her mad to be used like that. He was merely being nice so he could trick her into doing his bidding, like doing his homework, his chores, or whatever. Margo could not understand why her mother allowed this behavior to go on, but she sure noticed the disparities between the ways she and her brother were raised, even at a very young age. Margo realized then that boys were favored, praised, and adored by both fathers and mothers. Boys could do no wrong.

"Oh he's just being a boy, and boys will be boys," her mother would smile when her brother punched her a good one in the arm. Margo heard her mother say that more than once as she was growing up, and he would run over her with his bicycle or push her down a flight of stairs, all in play of course. Margo could only come to the conclusion that her mother had been treated the same way.

Back in the day, women catered to the needs of the males in the family because they needed them to provide a roof over their heads, medical decisions and monetary support. When a man could have you committed to an insane asylum and you knew that, you did cater to his every whim. As Margo grew up, she came to believe that boys were spoiled and given leeway when it came to bad behavior toward girls. Margo thought boys got a pass because parents were so afraid that their boy could turn out to be gay, god forbid. Margo wanted to break the mold. She had seen how women in families always took the backseat where males were concerned. Males always had the floor and the women shut up, turned their attention to him, and listened when in their company. Margo had learned that generally in all countries and all cultures that through the centuries men have entrapped women in subservient positions.

Women had to fight over a hundred years to get the right to vote, and that came only after the black man got his vote first. Men's needs were always placed first, ahead of women's needs. Medicines were tested on men but also prescribed to women according to the results of the men's tests. It was men who ruled religions and government and therefore social norms. So of course they would place themselves, especially the almighty white males, above women and other minorities.

In the sixties when all the hype was the race to beat the Russians to the moon, Margo kept hearing that boys were so much better at mathematics than girls; and that girls should stick with housework, cooking, doing the laundry and raising babies. It was only revealed many years later in a movie called "Hidden Figures" that four black women were the math geniuses behind the calculations that carried the white astronauts to the moon in 1969. It was never revealed at the time when it was happening. Just male propaganda that males were better at math than females, which of course proved not to be true.

Margo thought back to when she was much younger.

At the time she did not really want to get married, but all her friends were excited about meeting the love of their lives and planning big weddings. Parents pushed girls to marry young as they were concerned about their status in society. Everyone wants to fit into social norms, no one wants to be left out. These were the social standards, and why parents did not want their daughters to be left out to become pitiful old maids, god forbid. Young males knew they were put on a pedestal, and girls would fall all over them as they did Elvis and the Beatles, just because they were males. Of course the crying, screaming young girls were staged, but still it set the social norm, and young women across the country jumped on the bandwagon. Girls easily followed suit, those screaming fans were probably told to scream their heads off and of course, they obeyed. Margo saw nothing in these male entertainers; all she saw was their male privilege.

Males were the ones who choose who their wife would be. He asked the girl of his choice out. A girl was to feel honored that he wanted to be with her. And of course, fathers and mothers pushed to get their daughters married to fit in with social standards. It was always a relief to parents when it came to getting their daughters married, and put under another man's thumb of monetary support, to love, honor and obey. They had to, for their livelihoods were provided by their husbands as she had no means of making a decent livable wage.

Margo did not want to follow the crowd but fell into

line to not disappoint her parents and to fit in, although her intuition told her differently. Why should men be praised, privileged, and given free rein to explore and take on adventures while women were trapped in what seemed to Margo as servitude positions. Women were to love, honor, obey and be cheerleaders for their men. Her social duty was to devote her life to him and put her dreams and wishes to the back of her mind, because as an individual she did not matter. Margo believed that men set medical, educational, political, religious, and societal norms for women that suited men's needs and the hell with hers. She had finally seen the light and the truth of the male authoritarian ways.

By the time Margo got into high school she realized that society puts men and women into categories and certain roles. Religion, the government, news media and magazines, and movies all depict women needing to be under a man's control in servant status. Of course men were in charge of all these principles. So a woman did not stand a chance to rise up beyond her servitude and dependent status in a marriage. She was sad about the unequal status of women in an apparent man's world.

Margo thought perhaps back in the pioneer days, gender roles were sufficient and understandable, life was brutal but simpler then. In modern times though Margo thought that the slave mentality of men did not work. In many cases, women became the brains behind the man, being careful to watch her words and make sure that he thought her ideas were his own to begin with. She made sure he won games, arguments and so on, in order to build his confidence, and the hell with hers. Margo got the feeling that men thought women were put on Earth to morally, mentally and silently stay behind the scenes and support her man while he got all the glory for her ideas. *Why?* Margo thought! She was tired of taking the backseat to men all her life, as if they were the fragile ego ones, and of course, they were. She was not going to take it anymore. None of the things male rulers and corporate heads did made sense to Margo. *Why poison the air, water, food?* she thought.

Being a hybrid from Pleiades, Margo got sort of an outsiders view at the way human beings conducted their lives. She mostly observed the behavior of the male population. She watched and thought, of course men think they are gods because they alone pull the strings of government, mess with the economy, choose peace, war or fathom. So of course, their actions seem god like. And for now, Margo would still be forced to go with the flow of this male dominated world. Big changes were coming to her though.

In Margo's Astrological birth chart her sun was in the Zodiac sign of Taurus and very grounded, so she was slow to accept change. She did not want to leave her house. This was her house too, but she was going to have to leave it all behind and just disappear—for a while anyway.

Margo was frightened of her husband finding her in their house after he came back from her funeral. But as soon as Joe left, the Valium that he gave her suddenly took effect and she fell into a deep sleep and laid curled up on the couch. She was fast asleep and as she dreamed of Sara, a bright light woke her up.

And suddenly Sara appeared before her like the Blessed Virgin, Sara thought. Sara appeared extended about a foot above the floor and floated about the room. The bright light that surrounded her soon woke up Margo. Seeing Sara again reaffirmed and convinced Margo that she was not dreaming or going crazy.

Chapter Fifteen

Sara floated about the room. Margo was amazed at how Sara defied gravity as she did. She had to ask her how it was done.

"So how do you do that?" asked Margo slowly opening her eyes and seeing Sara floating above the floor. She wondered if she could ever be able to do that. She was amazed by Sara and admired her. She was beautiful, dressed in silky shinny hooded one piece suit much like what Margo was wearing.

"Do what my dear?" asked Sara with an inquisitive look but knowing exactly what Margo was referring to.

"Float above the floor like that," answered Margo wondering if she would ever be able to do that, "just how do you do that?"

Sara had an opaque appearance about her and almost always in a spiritual form; as if she could not quite get fully into human form. Sara was of the dawning of the Age of Aquarius the fifth dimension, ruled by the feminine energy of Pleiades star system. She was a

Pleiadian. Sara had to lower her frequency vibrations a bit to present herself to Margo. It was the dawning of the Fifth Dimension of planet Earth, so she had to transform herself in order to appear on Earth, which was exiting the fourth dimension, the age of Pisces, ruled by the Anunnaki Reptilian authoritarian rule, ascendants of Mars.

Sara floated about the room rather than taking actual steps. Margo noticed the crew of ladies on the spacecraft appeared to silently move about in the same fashion. She had felt the odd one out when she was among them, being the only one shorter than the rest on board because she took actual noisy steps.

"I will explain it to you later my dear. We need to go now," ordered Sara.

Sara had no time to explain to Margo how she could float above the floor. It was time to get Margo out of the house as Jack was on his way there. They were going to have to hurry.

"Get up dear, we need to be on our way," ordered Sara with a smile in a soft voice mentally nudging Margo's shoulder just a bit to arouse her.

"I was just thinking of you in my dream, and here you are," admitted Margo speaking slowly as she was still feeling the drowsy effects of the sedative.

"I know, I am always just a thought away," Sara said.

"Did you come in your silver saucer?" Margo dreamingly asked in a low voice not quite fully awake. She should have waited until she was someplace else;

someplace safe before taking that Valium. But she had taken what Joe had offered her because at that moment her nerves had felt raw and frayed. She was at her wits end and felt dazed and dopey now.

"Aren't you afraid Jack would come here and find you?" Sara asked sounding concerned.

"Well yes, but the sedative Joe gave me really knocked me out, I guess," answered Margo in a sleepy voice.

"Well, truth be told, we did have to distract Jack and steer him away from you for a while, so unfortunately someone's box of nails slide off the bed of their pickup truck onto the roadway. And, unfortunately Jack had followed the truck rather closely and had no time to swerve and miss the scattered nails that were all over the pavement. Jack had two flat tires and only one spare so that should delay him long enough to give you sufficient time to gather a few things and get out of here. We distracted him so we could come and get you so he wouldn't get here and find you asleep on the sofa. We think you would be dead for sure if that happened. Because for sure he would have to finish you off and gotten rid of your body. You see, to him you are dead, and you need to be dead. If he finds out you are still alive, he will kill you. We only have a short window of time for you to gather some things to take with you. Remember you are supposed to be dead. It's bad enough that your friend Joe found out about you still being alive," insisted Sara. Unlike Margo, clear headed Sara, without drugs in her system at the moment, sounded more concerned than Margo.

"You knew that?" asked Margo. She was so amazed by the likes of Sara and the other women like her.

"You saw what was going on and you could steer Jack away," asked Margo?

"Yes we can alter the future a bit, if we concentrate intently and use telepathy, we can change a human's mind," explained Sara. "We don't only fly our crafts with our minds, there is so much more we do with our minds. Humans can do this too, but unfortunately they are unaware because your governments, religions and medical corporate heads do not want you to know just how powerful your will and your mind really are. We are all connected to one mind, a universal mind where telepathy and thoughts creates reality," shared Sara.

"What do you mean?" asked Margo.

"Well, have you ever thought of someone you haven't heard from for a while, and then they call," asked Sara. "You can heal yourself too. Your thoughts and emotions cause illness and your thoughts and emotions can heal you. Your thoughts affect your immune system and with positive thoughts and emotions, they can heal and reverse an illness."

"That's amazing," sighed Margo.

"Come hurry," prompted Sara, "we need to get you out of here."

"You will teach me these things too, won't you?"

"Oh yes," confessed Sara, "in time my dear, in time," not fully ready to expose all of their mystical magical powers, just yet. In time Margo would learn all about them and she too would have the same powers when she becomes fully conscious of them.

"Well get me out of here then," suggested Margo eager to flee now, knowing that Jack may come through the door any minute.

"Come on, we know where there is a well stocked and comfortable little cabin for you to hide in for a while,"

"I'll grab my bag," replied a now eager Margo. "But first I am folding up these newspapers and putting them back on the driveway."

"Good thinking," smiled Sara.

Margo was ready to get out of there and away from the possibility of Jack coming to find her.

"Make sure the luggage or travel bag you choose to use is one that has been in the back of the closet, so Jack will not notice anything is missing or is out of place," suggested Sara.

"Good idea," Margo smiled in agreement and she immediately thought of a nice size luggage piece that she had not used for a while and was in the back of her closet under a bunch of other things she had not used in a while. Funny how closets get so junked up and cluttered she thought, pushing herself along, as she was still feeling very relaxed and still a little drugged from the sedative she took, but it had worn off some now and she paid attention to Sara's advice and hurried and got her things ready.

It did not take long for Margo to pack a few clothes and items of necessity.

"Come, hurry."

"Where's the silver saucer?" asked Margo.

"It is hovering in that open space right behind the garage," answered Sara, leading Margo through the kitchen, out the back door and down the porch steps, across the back yard and behind the garage. Quickly a beam of light took both Sara and Margo up and into the craft as it was rising up and away from the ground. Once inside the craft, Margo watched monitors of their movement and ground activity and saw that just as Sara maneuvered the craft up and away that Jack's car pulled into the driveway.

"Wow, that was close," admitted Margo breathing a sigh of relief and then turning her attention back to watch Sara fly the saucer.

Chapter Sixteen

Margo marveled at how Sara easily maneuvered the silent craft and off they went into the heavens in the silvery spacecraft. The craft lifted and shifted in several different directions. With sleek and swift movement, it did not take long before Sara gently set the craft down in a grassy meadow near the top of a pine tree covered mountain. In the midst of a wooded area was a large grassy meadow and on the edge of it stood a small log cabin with storybook fairytale appeal. Tall flowering clinging bushes surrounded the cabin. Pink and orange flowers swayed gently in the breeze in striking contrast to the dark weathered logs of the cabin.

Sara landed the craft ever so smoothly several yards away from the front door of the cabin. Sara and Margo departed the craft and looked around. Margo marveled at all the peaceful natural beauty of the area. She marveled at the wondrous sounds of nature, the wind through the pines sounded like ocean waves slapping a sandy shore, so soothing. Birds were singing. It was late evening and dusk was falling upon them. The night creatures were tuning up their vocal chords. Margo loved the sounds of the tree frogs and other creatures chatty rhythms, creating their own unique tunes. The stars lit up the night sky. Margo pointed out Orion's belt and not far from there, she pointed out the Pleiades star system where Alcyone was located in the Taurus constellation.

"It is so beautiful here, the cabin, the night sky." Margo looking up and all around the night sky said, "Look, the Milky Way."

"Yes, my dear, come let's see inside the cabin." Sara led Margo inside the small log cabin.

"Oh this place looks lovely. I know I will love it here, thank you so much for helping me." Margo was much appreciative. Being here would give her a bit of relaxation and a time to think about her plans for the future.

"Now, this is just between you and me, right?" ordered Sara. "I do not exist, remember?" Sara reminded Margo.

"Got it!" Margo smiled in delight. "And I do not exist either, right?"

They both burst into laughter. Margo could not help but think how fortunate she was to be alive and experiencing this magical, mystical, and wonderful moment.

"Come, Margo," suggested Sara, as she hurried Margo along leading her by the hand. She moved fast and Margo tried to keep up. Margo had to laugh because indeed it would have been a sight to behold if anyone saw Margo hanging onto Sara's hand and trying to keep up with her. Sara, appearing much taller, glided along with both feet about a foot above the floor, followed by Margo taking noisy quick steps trying to keep up with the hovering beauty before her.

"I don't even know why you wear those slipper-like shoes, when your feet never even touch the floor," smirked Margo having fun. She was getting to know Sara better know and felt comfortable joking with her.

"You're just jealous, I know." Sara knew that if Margo was a hybrid, she would probably be able to do the same things as Sara.

"You're right about that," sighed Margo, "yes, I am very jealous."

"Here look, what do you think so far?" asked Sara as she came to a halt so Margo could look around the cabin. She wanted to show Margo where she would be staying. She knew Margo would love it and she did.

Chapter Seventeen

Joe sat on the patio at a coffee shop where he had made arrangements to meet Jack. He anxiously awaited Jack's arrival as he sipped the strong hot coffee, it was soothing and warmed him in the chilly morning air. He had just hung up the phone with his lawyers who were dealing with his wife's untimely wrongful death. A malicious toxic cancer treatment abruptly ended her life in an excruciating painful way, instead of helping her. Life had been very tough with worry and hurt. Joe wanted to escape the sharp pain of reality, and he dreamed of using the settlement money to leave town for a while and get away from it all.

Joe envied Jack's freedom of mind and thought he would like to be more like Jack and knew that he was, in a way. Joe admired Jack and was beginning to figure out Jack's ways and adhere to them himself. Perhaps it was in their blood as Jack and Joe were cousins. Joe was beginning to think that Jack was turning out to be a ruthless homicidal maniac though, and Joe wondered if he should be cautious.

Joe became impatient waiting for Jack. He felt foolish, sitting there waiting for independent thinking Jack to show up. Jack who lived by his own social standards had his own time clock and schedule. Joe knew Jack would be running late as usual, as he was already ten minutes late.

While he waited for Jack to get there, Joe enjoyed hot black brew that he knew he shouldn't have because it would make him even more anxious. But he couldn't resist the rich aroma that permeated the air around the coffee shop. He so enjoyed the rich sweet bitterness of it and the sudden buzz. The bitter taste on his tongue matched his mood. Joe was getting even more impatient waiting for Jack to show up, he began tapping his foot nervously.

Finally, Joe saw Jack come strolling around the corner as if he had all day. He watched him as he walked through the black rod iron gate and passed through the vine covered patio fence. Joe sat at a table near the fence under the wide thick canopy of a huge oak tree. Jack saw Joe and nodded in greeting as he walked up to the table. In one swift motion he pulled out the big heavy medal chair and flopped down, slouching in the chair, he felt as tired as he knew he looked. He had not gotten much sleep since the accident and then with all the funeral arrangements, working with the life insurance claims' department, and now he was dealing with getting the house cleared out and set up to sell.

"It's about time you got here," harped Joe in his usual impatient tone.

"What is this place anyway, and why so far out of the way?"

"I just felt like taking a drive," sneered Joe slowly lifting his coffee cup to his lips to take another much needed sip. It was difficult for Joe to keep a secret no matter what or who he promised, nor the circumstances, so he had to bite his tongue. Joe got to the point where he was going to tell Jack that Margo was alive, but suddenly decided not to. *Who knows, maybe blackmail would come in handy one day,* he thought. So Instead of the secret about Margo being alive, Joe decided to tell Jack that he wanted to ask him for the money he owed him. While Jack was busy with funeral arrangements, Joe had taken Jack's damaged truck to the repair shop. Joe used his own cash so Jack needed to repay him and owed him a few grand. Joe decided that would be his only reason for telling Jack why he wanted to meet up with him.

"Who's alive?" snapped Jack suddenly turning and looking all around with a frightened look on his face.

"I said, I felt like taking a drive," Joe repeated quickly and louder as he was trying very hard not to burst out loud with laugher at Jack's prominent display of a guilty conscience.

"Oh, it's all that chatter around us," Jack explained with a very worried look. He was edgy since he had just buried an innocent stranger in Margo's place.

Joe saw how shook-up Jack was and decided maybe

he could easily blackmail Jack after all. He would have to ponder that thought.

"And yes, Jack, you just said it yourself that your wife is alive," Joe said with a knowing look in his eyes. In a way, Joe's pride forced him to give Jack just a hint to let him know that he knew the truth. After all, why should it all be so easy for Jack to get away with his sinister crimes?

"Just what are you talking about. Margo died in the accident and was buried," smirked Jack. "You are beginning to sound like you lost your mind Joe." Jack knew he had to cut Joe off quickly before his accusations went any further.

"So Jack, who is the woman who was buried?" Joe repeated. He was convinced that he was not losing his mind and now getting a little mad at the suggestion he was going nuts, he wanted to give Jack some grief.

"What? I can't believe this," snorted Jack with anger in his voice. He thought this whole mess was all wrapped up. He was ready to head out of town with the two million dollars he collected from the life insurance policy and begin a new life. He had done this before with his first and second wives, and both events went off without a hitch, no one suspected, not even his suspicious cousin, Joe, who looked at him now like he was from another planet.

Jack schemes worked in the past as both times he moved to another state afterward to begin anew. But he came back to his hometown for a visit between wives and that is where he met Margo, a real estate agent. He had seen her picture and read that she won an excellence award for selling the most million dollar homes in the county. So Jack had followed her and watched her from afar as she went about her work days. Sometimes he would attend the open houses in order to engage her in conversation. He had seen the attractive real estate agent putting up the open house sign and wanted to engage her in conversation. She was very attractive, and he was intrigued and so he decided to pull over and take a look at the house and meet this lovely lady, perhaps she would be his next wife.

Jack wanted to meet her outside of home viewing so he got bold but knew he did wrong when he punctured her tire with an ice pick. He followed from a distance until the tire went totally flat and she pulled over. He pulled up behind her and parked, got out of his car and walked up to hers and offered to help her. Margo was on her way to see a client and was running late as it was, so she happily accepted his offer to change her flat tire. As luck would have it, Jack felt as if they hit it off as she wore no wedding ring and appeared to be attracted to him. Conversation came easily and so Jack asked Margo out for lunch. And that is how Margo got to know Jack; they dated for a very short time before he proposed marriage.

Chapter Eighteen

Jack did have a bit of a guilty conscious, it even surprised him, that he did feel the slight pang of remorse in his gut. But it seems he always did after the deed; after all, the ladies were pleasant and nice all in all, but business was business. Actually, he was beginning to wonder if it hadn't become a kind of thrilling addiction to him. He always got an adrenaline rush after the deed was done and the check came in the mail.

Margo was his third wife and third victim. He liked Margo okay after they were married; in his own selfish childish way he even loved her. But as time went on, Margo got on Jack's nerves. Or was he just getting restless? It was time to move on, collect life insurance policy money and then move on to find his next victim. And so he forced his own wife's car off the road that night down the embankment into the flooded water. Jack drove away then and went home. It took him a while to work up the courage to go back to the scene of the crime and climb down the muddy embankment into the flooded water to find her body and call the authorities to retrieve her body from the wrecked car.

He went back and parked his truck on the side of the road where he saw the muddy ruts and skids of tire tracks. He got out of the truck and headed to the water to look for Margo's body in the wreckage. It was muddy. He slipped and slid and grabbed and hung onto branches as he slowly crept down the muddy embankment. He spotted the overturned nearly submerged vehicle. He waded in almost waist deep water to get to the car. He saw the busted outside window and with his flashlight shining brightly he waded into the murky waters. He searched the car and poked around the dark areas with a long stick and saw and felt nothing. Where was she? His guess was that her body somehow drifted out the broken window as there was a pretty swift current. The current was swift enough that he had to hang on to the car to keep from being pulled and swept away. He gave up when he could not find her and figured that the current must have taken her away and probably wild animals got to her. The flooded area flowed along the road and went on for miles until it emptied into a big creek which eventually joined the river. Her body could be long gone by now. He was disturbed because he needed a body for a funeral and in order to collect the life insurance money. And then he got an idea.

He had been hanging out in a diner at the other end of town and chatting it up with the new waitress there who said she was new in town. He would sit at the counter and visit with her during the slow times when she worked. They got pretty chummy. He told her he was an over the road truck driver that was off work for a few days while his rig was worked on. One evening when she was in the diner alone closing up he dropped by to offer her a ride home so she would not have to walk alone in the dark.

He drove her to the flooded high water near the creek where his wife's car was submerged to show her the rising flood waters. She was amazed at how high the water was getting and flooding everything. When she turned to look out the passenger side window, he took the opportunity that presented itself and quickly reached for the hammer he had put on the floor behind her seat. She never knew what hit her. She was out cold, just the way he had planned it. He carried her down to the river. He hurried because it appeared as if she was coming to as she began to moan. He hurried and walked into the water's edge and submerged her body and held her under the murky water until she stopped moving and laid limp in his arms. She had water in her lungs and that was what he needed so it would appear that she drowned in the car wreck. He carefully moved her body to where his wife's wrecked car was mostly submerged and placed her inside through the broken out driver side window. He found the cut framed seat belt and wrapped it around her neck to keep her in place so she would not drift out of the car as apparently his wife's body did. For a moment he was puzzled to find that the seat belt was frayed, and torn but he did not have time to dwell on that and just wrapped it around her neck. He hurried then and scrambled back up the embankment. When he got back up to the road as luck would have it, a state trooper was driving by, and Jack managed to flag the trooper down. He threw himself on the ground on his hands and knees and pounded the pavement as he cried and carried on.

"Why, why," he moaned. It was raining again so he did not have to worry about generating fake tears. He tearfully told the trooper that he found his wife's car and her body submerged in deep water and that he needed help to get her out. The trooper called it in and got an ambulance for the body and a wrecker to the scene to pull the submerged car out of the water. The woman's body was identified by Jack as his wife Margo.

"Oh, my Margo," He cried and carried on and there were no questions from the police, the coroner or anyone. Jack loved the attention, the drama and the way people easily fell for his tragic stories. People see what they expect to see or what they want to see, and he relied on that. The plan was easily put into motion now.

It had been a trying time for Jack and after the funeral he was feeling pretty caught up in stress and felt on edge. By the time Jack caught up with Joe for coffee that morning his nerves were raw from all the uncertainties and risks he had undertaken in the last few days. The whole ordeal was working on his nerves and he was feeling more than a little jumpy. So when Joe said he wanted money, Jack forgot about Joe using his own money to pay for getting his damaged truck fixed and thought that he was just being used.

"Oh Jack, I believe you know what I want," insisted Joe sitting up straight in his chair and ready to get down to business details. In his head he figured about how much Jack owed him for the dented truck repair, as he had forgotten to bring the invoice along with him.

"You want part of the life insurance money, I suspect," replied Jack "Well that is not going to happen. You cannot blackmail me for something that has not happened." Jack was nervous and so he was mumbling.

"What?" asked Joe. He really wanted to just laugh out loud at the guilty sounding comments Jack nervously made. It was plain to see the tension of his wrong doings were mounting.

"Sure, I'll take your money, if you want to share it, of course, but I was merely going to ask you for the money you owe me for getting your dented truck repaired. Remember that I did that for you. I paid for it with my own money, remember? I took care of that for you while you were busy making funeral arrangements." Joe was making sure Jack knew that he went out of his way to help him.

"You must be losing your mind," Jack swore in a low voice as to not be over heard. Jack spoke as if he did not hear what Joe had just said about only wanting to be reimbursed the money he used for getting the dented truck repaired.

"What do you mean losing my mind? I used my own cash to get your dented truck fixed, that is all that I am asking of you," Joe angrily shot right back at Jack then went on in a softer more realistic voice as to not attract attention from people sitting at surrounding tables. "Jack, I only want the money you owe me for getting your truck fixed," Joe repeated.

"Oh, okay then," Jack said nervously. He knew that he had to be careful to control the anger in his voice as he was thinking that there was no way he would split the insurance money with Joe since he took all the risks. Joe could be dealt with the same way that he dealt with Margo and the waitress. In all the confusion, Jack had forgotten that he asked Joe to take his pickup and get it fixed while he was busy with funeral arrangements. At the time, Jack had told Joe that he drove too close and sideswiped a fence post. The damaged fender rubbed on the tire, so it needed to get fixed right away because he could not drive it that way. He did not want to further damage the tire and hated driving a dented truck and since Jack was busy, Joe agreed to take it and get it fixed for him.

Seeing Jack all shook up now, Joe wanted to play with Jack's psychic really badly. He had had thoughts of blackmailing Jack but thought differently of it and decided to wait. He felt that he could always blackmail Jack if and whenever he wanted to. But in his head he played out the scenario if he confronted Jack, and then he thought, *Oh the hell with it, think I'll torment him further since he is a wreck already.*

"I know what I saw," sneered Joe with an evil smirk on his face. "I saw Margo back at your house, and she was alive and kicking." Joe was flippant and figured if Jack had nerve enough to do what he did, kill for money, then he had sufficient nerve to blackmail him.

"She's dead and buried, Joe," insisted Jack, "and I think your mind just has a strange way of processing the fact that she is gone; that she died in that horrible car crash. Maybe you are psychic and she appeared to you in spirit."

Joe could tell that he was getting nowhere with Jack. Jack was not taking the bait and Joe actually began to feel that he was losing his mind.

"Well, you'll see." Joe wasn't quit giving up yet.

"I think you need help, Joe I think you are losing it."

If it were true, that Margo was still alive then Jack suspected that Margo and Joe were working together against him. Jack's mind went into a frenzy of suspicious scenarios. Subconsciously Jack felt everyone was as underhanded and crooked as he was, and so he did not believe or trust anyone. Jack had the insurance money now and he had plans to head out of town, pronto. The sooner the better, he thought.

"Oh yeah, you'll see her again one day," smiled Joe mischievously.

"What, you really expect me to believe that?" Jack could only hope that Joe was bluffing.

"Of course," smirked Joe, feeling confident and sure of himself.

"I think you need to go home and sleep off whatever you are on these days," suggested Jack.

Jack was smart enough not to let on, but he was

becoming rather nervous. So there was a fly in the ointment, and the fly's name was Joe. It could have been the perfect crime if not for Joe. Either Jack had to take the money and run now or stick around a bit longer and get rid of Joe.

"Think about it, Jack," suggested Joe, "I want the money tomorrow, or I will go to the authorities."

"No way," Jack said in a silent rage. He wanted to punch Joe in the face, or better yet do him in, cousin or no cousin. Instead, Jack watched in astonishing wonder as Joe let him sit there in silence and got up and headed out to the parking lot. Jack did not believe Joe's story about Margo being alive, he thought Joe was trying to pull one over on him in order to get part or half of the life insurance money that Jack received.

"Go to hell," sneered Jack through his teeth after sitting in silence for a few minutes watching Joe walk away. In a fit of rage Jack jumped up and as he did kicked the chair to the ground causing a racket. People around him turned to see what was going on. Jack had forgotten about the people sitting all around him, so he collected himself, picked up the chair and set it upright. He felt embarrassed and conspicuous, so he walked out of there fast and headed to his truck. Joe had indeed sparked a curious frantic reaction in Jack and he had to find out for himself. So Joe hung around the corner and watched Jack get into his pickup and drive off.

Chapter Nineteen

Jack drove like crazy to the house. He drove over the old and newly delivered newspapers lying in the driveway. He slammed on the brakes, shut off the engine, and raced up to the front door. He quickly unlocked it and burst into the house. He searched high and low and could not find any trace of Margo anywhere. He was furious at Joe for pulling this stunt on him. But still Jack wondered, *could Margo indeed be alive?*

Joe successfully had planted the thought in Jack's mind that somehow Margo got out of the wreckage and the rising flood water and was still alive. Jack looked in every room and every closet and to him nothing had changed or was misplaced. Everything was s it had been. Her clothes and everything were still there, nothing seemed to have been changed or misplaced. Jack wondered why on earth would Joe say such a thing about Margo still being alive?

He just couldn't figure it out. He wondered if Joe was playing games with him. Was Jack losing his mind? Jack still tried to convince himself that animals indeed got to

Margo's body and dragged it off. Jack believed that no matter what Joe tried to tell him. He soon forgot about what Joe had said, he had important and immediate things to take care of before leaving town. Jack thought the heck with Joe and began to make calls in order to get the house cleared out and in preparation to put on the market.

Chapter Twenty

"It's so beautiful here," Margo said looking around at the lovely natural panoramic views that surrounded her. From the mountain top clearing where she sat, she could see in all directions, endless wooded beauty. Sara and Margo had landed onto a beautiful grassy, wooded area surround by mountains of tall pine trees and rocky cliffs. They could hear the relaxing sound of spring water flowing down from the mountain through the rocky creek that flowed behind the cabin.

"How do you like the cabin?" asked Sara, already knowing the answer as she saw the smile on Margo's face, which warmed her heart. All Pleiadians had extreme psychic intuitive mind reading skills. Pleiadians as hybrid humans are spiritual beings existing on Earth and other planets and galaxies in various forms of life presenting human like qualities. Throughout the universe, our minds, souls and consciousness are all one and the same. We are all connected via our minds, souls, and consciousness. Our bodies may wear out and die, but our souls live on. It's why our passed loved ones are just a thought away. Our love and thoughts of them keep them close and protecting us. One does not have to be an empathic psychic medium to connect with a passed loved one, just think of them, they are just a thought away, and they will be with you. They know what is going on with you so talk to them. All humans on Earth are hybrids because we all come from the stars. But Sara knew that some Pleiadian Hybrids such as Margo, have a little harder time realizing all of their gifts as many were not aware till much later in life that they were hybrids.

"It is very charming," answered Margo, "and it looks so cozy, I can't wait to see the rest of it."

"Come, my dear," Sara smiled taking the lead, "walk this way."

"Easy for you to say," smiled Margo watching Sara moving ahead of her floating across the room.

Margo had to laugh as she could barely keep up with the tall beauty. She held tightly to Sara's hand as Sara floated above the floor and led the way. The cabin was indeed warm and cozy. It was well furnished, and the cupboards were filled with toiletries, towels, and just everything Margo might need. The kitchen cabinets and refrigerator were well stocked with all the things that Margo loved. She was impressed. *How did they know to have all the things there that she liked*, Margo wondered.

"It's furnished beautifully. How did you get all these things up here on this mountain?" Margo was very pleased.

"Spacecraft and drone," replied Sara.

"Of course," Margo mused. It just seemed to Margo that Sara and the Pleiadians had it all figured out as to how to live an efficient designed existence. They were so organized. The cabin was wonderful, but Margo felt pulled to Alcyone. She wanted to go back and stay there. Alcyone was so futuristically designed, clean, and quiet. No wars, no crimes, no violence. Everyone got along and came together for the greater good of all citizens on Alcyone . Alcyone was a retreat, whereas it seemed to Margo that Earth was a conflict of various harmful ideals, racism, misogynistic behavior, wars, greed, theft, and jealousy. Margo wanted to leave that all behind. She had heard Earth was a learning place where souls incarnated to learn and advance. Margo thought, *why? Leave it behind. Its where all the Martians landed after they destroyed their planet, Mars, and made it inhabitable.*

"Thank you for coming to my rescue. I love you for it," Margo flopped onto the sofa. She was suddenly very tired.

"I'll leave you to it now," sighed Sara, "make yourself comfortable and if you need anything, remember I am just a thought away."

"This is so generous of you," Margo was practically in tears being filled with gratitude. She did not know where her next permanent home would be; but in the interim, this cabin was perfect for her. She laid there napping for a while. After a few minutes she woke up feeling hungry. She went to the kitchen and looked around the well stocked cupboards and refrigerator. She found a package of ground beef in the meat tray and got a box of spaghetti and jar of spaghetti sauce from the cupboard. While her dinner was cooking, she looked over the many metaphysical books and picked a good one to read while she ate dinner by candlelight with a glass of wine.

The next day she continued searching through the shelves that lined the living-room next to the fireplace, she spent an hour opening several books and looking through them. She would find a good one and read it while eating the grilled cheese sandwich and cream of tomato soup she made for lunch. She read for hours learning all about metaphysical theories, about meditating and sitting in power to connect with her spirit guides. There was much there to read and learn and she wanted to learn it all. She was fascinated by spiritual metaphysical phenomena, for example how powerful our thoughts are, and how they can keep us well, make us sick, and make us well again. Disease happens when our emotions are stressed and compromised; but if we can eliminate the cause and the reason for the stress, then we can learn to heal ourselves.

The dining and living-room areas were decorated in warm colors and felt very cozy. Margo felt very much at home. The cabin felt warm and calming, just what Margo needed for now. She did not feel alone, knowing her spirit guides were with her and that Sara was just a thought away.

Margo was engrossed in an interesting metaphysical

book. As she read though a bit of uneasiness creeped up in her. Did she hear noises outside, wild animals perhaps. She became a little worried. Now, she wasn't only afraid of Jack finding her she was also afraid of Joe finding her, too. She believed since Joe knew she was still alive, that by now he had told Jack. Joe and Jack were cousins, she assumed blood was thicker than water, as the saying goes.

Joe had been a friend but now she no longer trusted him after he gave her that super charged sedative that would have knocked her out for hours if Sara not have come along to wake her up. And she wondered, *did Joe give her the strong sedative so she would be there for Jack to find?* The more she thought about it, the more she was beginning to have negative feelings about Joe.

Margo realized the dire straits she had been in, she could have easily died in the car wreck. She was very grateful that Sara had come along to help her out. It was better she thought, that she stayed hidden for a while, at least until Sara could tell her that the coast was clear and help her plan her next move.

No matter what, like it or not, Margo was about to begin a new life; but, for now anyway, she would remain out of sight and off the grid. She mourned her former life. She was dead to everyone now. The Real Estate agency she worked for had buried her too. Her accounts and her desk were taken over by a fellow agent, Margo's friend, Claire.

Chapter Twenty-One

Jack finally decided Joe was playing a trick on him. Soon he forgot about Joe saying he saw Margo as he needed to get busy and finish getting the house set up to sell. He would not rest easy until a realtor had it listed and then he could leave town. In the meantime, he was very busy and hired help to clear out everything from the house, giving most of the stuff to charity. He had called a realtor and the house was on the market. He was free to leave town now and was all packed and ready to leave the scene of the crime and escape to another state. Florida sounded very good to him.

He had enough money to live anywhere. He had not been to Florida and figured that the Miami area should have the richest divorcees and widows of anywhere, so he headed there. Besides winter was on its way and Florida would be a nice warm change. He booked a suite at one of Palm Beach's fanciest resorts and after he arrived and got settled in his room, he headed to the cabana bar on the beach for drinks.

Jack smiled with confidence as he felt very confident and just simply knew that the lovely lady sitting at the bar sipping on one of those fancy drinks with an umbrella sticking out of it could easily fall for his charming personality. He was so confident he could turn on the charm and win her over. He knew he was a handsome guy as the ladies always told him he was. He had a dazzling smile and could be very warm and engaging. He counted on these talents to attract his targets of unsuspecting lonely ladies and so he asked the woman sitting at the resort bar this obvious over-used and laughable ice breaker. He cozied up to the bar, a bar stool distance apart from the first rich looking lovely woman he saw sitting alone.

"Come here often?" asked Jack as he smiled at the lovely lady.

Jack was wasting no time as he was on the prowl and ready to search for his next potential victim. He had enough money for now anyway and he did not need to entrap another wealthy woman into marriage, but the excitement and intrigue was in his blood having had three successful encounters under his belt. So he was eager to meet his fourth wife. Having gotten away with murder for life insurance money several times in several states he was hooked and wanted to test is luck and see if he could get away with another one; he was pretty confident that he could. He wanted a really rich victim this time, a lovely lady who could match the millionaire lifestyle he had adopted.

"You bet," smiled the lovely lady holding up her martini glass in a saluted hello gesture.

The lovely lady sitting at the bar looked very rich indeed. She was dressed in fancy jeweled strapped sandals and royal blue swim clothes with matching floral jacket. He nails and lips painted the same shade of strawberry red. Under her hat, her hair hung with beautiful thick blonde curls down to her shoulders. Jack smiled and nodded at this very attractive blue-eyed beauty and thought that this new adventure was going to be fun.

"Hi, the name is Jack," he smiled holding out his hand to her.

"Judy," she replied with a warm smile taking his hand gently for a moment. She welcomed his presence as she thought he seemed nice and was handsome indeed.

"Hi, it's nice to see a friendly face," Judy said as Jack approached her smiling. She used her best flirty smile, but not too flirty. *A little mystery and intrigue never hurt,* she thought. Judy was on a mission. She had been recently widowed and was determined to turn her lonely life around. She was self-confident knowing that she was very attractive. She was on a mission to find a man to suit her needs.

"Hi, likewise, mind if I sit?" He motioned to the bar stool next to where she sat.

"Oh, please do," replied Judy. She sat facing the ocean, watching the waves slap the sandy shore, as she sipped a vodka martini. She was beginning to feel the effects of the potent drink in the fancy glass before her. She was halfway down and thinking about getting another.

Jack asked what she was drinking. It looked deliciously refreshing and ordered one .

"Would you like another?" offered Jack watching her take another sip and pointing at her now nearly empty glass.

"Well, I shouldn't, but thank you, I think I will. Remind me to drink the next one much slower as this one I drank rather quickly and it went straight to my head," she laughed a contagious laugh that pulled Jack in and he had to laugh too. In a minute the bartender smiled and carefully sat two full to the brim vodka martinis in front of them. The glass was so full that they both had to lower their heads to get down and sneak up on it and take tiny sips until it was safe to pick it up without spilling any of the precious concoction. They both laughed at their awkwardness. So for the next few minutes they entertained everyone sitting at the bar. They both laughed as they carefully took a sips and watched the bartender join in the laughter as well as the other patrons sitting across from them at the horseshoe shaped bar.

"Oh, my, this is delicious," commented Jack. "It is hard not to just drink it down all at once."

"Oh, you may not want to do that," Judy said and they both laughed.

It was apparent to the bartender and everyone sitting around them that Jack and Judy immediately hit it off. They were all smiles and undivided attention as they talked amongst themselves. They shared stories about their recent arrivals, where they were staying and how they found their accommodations. Finally they got around to talking about their past spouses who had coincidentally both recently passed. Judy said her husband died from a heart attack, and Jack said his wife died in a car accident.

The horseshoe shape thatched roof cabana bar was located a short walk from the hotel on the beach, it was a lovely venue. A cool ocean breeze ruffled their hair, and a gust lift Judy's wide brim hat and sent it tumbling down the beach. Judy had to laugh watching the boyish image of Jack, jumping off the barstool and running down the beach after it. His long curly sun-streaked brown hair whipping in the wind. His unbuttoned shirt tails flying as he darted back and forth every which way the hat jerked about on the sand. He was tempted to stomp on it, to hold it in place. He thought she might be watching; but thought the hell with it and when he had the chance, he pounced down hard with his left foot when he got the chance to trap the hat.

"My hero," Judy laughed when Jack returned out of breath, dented hat in hand, and handed it to her. They both laughed. She gave him a big hug. Everyone else at the bar laughed along with them. The bartender smiled as he set a fresh drink down for each of them, "on the house."

The sound and view of the surf was so beautiful and relaxing and could be seen from any bar stool no matter where you sat. The bar was neatly decorated with an inviting Polynesia style thatched roof with dried grassy fringe that hung down and swayed to and fro in the ocean breeze. The mood was light, warm, and they were drunk with drink, each other and a wonderful view, all of which invited romance. A spell was cast between them, that made the drinking, chatting, and the afternoon magical. An alluring sensual mood complimented the effects the vodka martinis. The weather was perfect. Jack was pleased with the company he shared and apparently she was too, as they both lingered the afternoon away and lost track of time. Before they realized it, hours had passed. This woman, he thought, could easily win his heart. He wanted to learn all he could about her.

"Besides being a lovely resort, what brings you here, if you do not mind me asking?" inquired Jack

"Well, I guess you could say a change in my life brought me here. You could say that I am closing one chapter and opening another."

"That's sounds interesting, I guess I am too," Jack said.

"Do tell," she prompted.

"Well, I have been grieving the passing of my wife." Jack kept his head lowered for a moment in fake sad devotion. Tried to act like he was about to cry, but by now he had had enough to drink that he really wanted to laugh out loud, a big hardy laugh instead.

"Oh, that is so sad. Loss of a loved one is so difficult to bear," sympathized Judy, "I guess I have a somewhat similar story. My husband and I had this vacation planned for over three years. We kept putting it off because of his demanding work. And then suddenly one day he had a heart attack and he died instantly without warning. It was devastating to me. So just goes to show, you never know."

"Oh no, that is so sad," sympathized Jack, "I am sorry for your loss." He had to control himself not to smile-- this was a sad moment. But in his mind he was glad that she was single. He thought she was perfect for him.

"Yes very sad, so after the funeral and after all the things got settled, I decided to come anyway on the vacation we had planned together," confessed Judy.

"Might as well," sided Jack.

"I just needed to get away and decide in which direction my life will go on from here," added Judy.

"I know what you mean," nodded Jack, "it's tough life is so full of twists and turns,"

"So I am at the crossroads of life, I guess you could say." Judy enjoyed talking to this good-looking man who seemed to be going through the same thing she had been going through. It was nice to have someone to commiserate with at this time in her life. She had been hesitant to vacation on her own, but then considered this trip a retreat of sorts to just relax, go to the spa, read a book, and enjoy the beauty of the area; but this, this was an exciting added plus. Her husband always told her that he never wanted her to be alone if something were ever to happen to him. He wanted her to be happy. He had always taken good care of her and even after his death left her financially secure and she was most grateful for that.

"I know what you mean," said Jack, "we all need to do what we each individually need to do for ourselves."

Jack thought this scenario was perfect. She said that she was from Memphis, he had never lived in the state of Tennessee. He was interested and thought that a new place where no one knew him would be an ideal scenario. It would be a state where insurance companies would have no real reason to check too deeply into his background being a widow on three previous occasions. Jack always moved to another state and used small life insurance companies with local offices not affiliated nationwide.

To Jack it appeared that Judy had lots of money as she spoke of her deceased husband being an investment manager who ran his own investment firm very profitably. Judy was attractive, sweet and he could tell already, good company, this adventure was going to be fun.

They had such a great time, that they decided to go back to their rooms clean up and meet at a popular Mexican restaurant close to their hotels. There they had delicious entrees, fine wine, desert and then sat and talked late into the evening. They walked barefoot along the beach in the moon light. It was so romantic. He walked her back to her hotel which was on the way to his; bid her a good night and asked her to dinner the next evening. He wanted to start out slow and easy; after all, she and he were grieving spouses. He could take his time with this one for the prize was high and very sufficient.

Chapter Twenty-Two

Joe sat at his desk at work pondering his next move regarding Jack. Joe was perplexed because he did not know what to do about the information he had which was threefold: First, Margo was not dead. Second: A Jane Doe, missing woman, perhaps the missing waitress written about in the newspaper, was buried in Margo's place and Three: Jack was the obvious perpetuator. Joe had all the necessary information. What should he do with this information? If he kept the information to himself would it be against the law? Would he be considered withholding evidence and therefore thought a co-conspirator, an accomplice in crime? Joe thought he was an accomplice if he did not inform the authorities. Joe worried about this as he went about his daily routines. He wanted to talk to Margo. After all he had no case without Margo as proof of evidence.

He decided to go to Jack and Margo's house to see if Jack was there. He could get the money Jack owed him

for getting the dented truck repaired since he jumped
up and stormed away without Jack paying him the last
time he saw him.

Chapter Twenty-Three

When Joe pulled up to Jack's house and parked on the street, he saw that neither Jack's truck nor car was there. There was one car in the driveway which looked like it belonged to the person hammering the for-sale sign in the ground in the front yard. Peering through his windshield in his parked car, Joe saw that the woman was very attractive. She had light brown shoulder-length hair and wore a white blouse, soft blue skirt, and a suit jacket. Joe sat in his car for a few minutes and watched her as she walked back into the house. He sat there for a few more minutes checking phone calls and emails and then decided to get out knock on the door and speak with her.

Claire, being a newly trained real estate agent, was concentrating on what she was doing. She had a checklist and was busy checking off items she needed to do for a sale. Margo had trained her. These were the items Margo had helped her with when it came time to stage a house for a sale. She went about her work, but it was very emotionally disturbing for her. She was in tears. She missed her mentor and good friend, Margo. It made it all the more depressing being in Margo's house and not having her be there. Margo was a wonderful friend, co-worker and mentor. Margo had been a good co-worker and taught her a lot when she first started at the agency. Claire was most grateful when she was hired and Margo took her under her wing and showed her the ropes of the business. As Claire wiped her tears away and went about her work getting the house ready to sell, she saw a man approach the front door. She had just put up the for sale sign out in front near the sidewalk.

"Hello, okay if I come in?" asked Joe, "I see you just put up the for sale sign."

"Hi, sure come on in," said the tearful real estate agent.

"Hi, my name is Joe and I just noticed the for sale sign."

"Hi, nice to meet you Joe. My name is Claire, yes, I am the real estate agent. I was a good friend of the woman who lived here, sorry for the tears," Claire explained to Joe who she thought was looking rather sad himself.

"I'm so sorry for your loss," Joe sympathized with her, "Margo was a friend of mine too, I knew her through her husband Jack. Jack's my cousin."

"I thought you looked familiar," said Claire.

"Yes, I thought the same of you, like maybe I met you at one of their luncheons or backyard barbecues but just can't place it for sure." said Joe,

"Yes, same with me," admitted Claire. She was glad to have the sudden interruption to help take her mind off Margo, if only for a few minutes.

They both agreed they had briefly met before. Claire proceeded to show him around the house and the small updated changes that had been made. As Joe looked around he was astonished that Jack had cleared everything out so fast and already had it on the market. Joe's attention easily turned back to Claire as he decided he wanted to get to know her better. He wondered if it would be too forward if he hung around and helped her.

Joe and Claire casually chatted about the real estate business. He immediately liked Claire and asked if he could help her as she was about to move a staging piece of furniture from one side of the living room to the other.

"I'll help you with that," offered Joe with a smile only too happy to help a sad woman grieve over the loss of her friend. He thought if only she knew that her friend, Margo, was still alive and kicking somewhere. Claire looked so sad he was near telling her when she asked for his help with moving some furniture around and help carry some boxes in from her car.

"I would appreciate that," Claire said as her eyes still filled with tears.

"I would be more than happy to help." Joe followed her out the front door to her car.

"The young college kid I usually have help me could not make it today," complained Claire, "so, I do thank you for your offer to help me."

Joe stayed for quite a while that afternoon, as Claire took full advantage of his offer to help her. She had him flex his muscles carrying in and emptying boxes of information flyers, lamps, tables, vases, and other things to get the house staged and ready for the upcoming weekend open house. They easily struck up conversations and it was plain to see that they both liked each other.

When it came time for Joe to leave, he asked if she would have dinner with him. He was happy to see her tear-stained face turn into a happy smile. He agreed to meet her at her office later in the day. Since it was such a pretty day, if it was okay with her, they could walk around the corner to a popular restaurant close to her work.

Joe was so excited about having met Claire and having a date with her that his mind could not settle down. He had been alone far too long. He had not felt like dating anyone but there was something different about Claire, and he was very attracted to her and he hoped she was to him. He decided he would walk around town a bit before it was time to meet up with her. He was in a daze not only about having a date with a lovely lady; but, also in a slight daze about trying to figure out what he was going to do about Jack. As he strolled about town, he looked for Jack, but there was no sign of him at the coffee shop or any of the other usual places he would frequent.

Chapter Twenty-Four

The cabin was lovely and comforting, and Margo was fine for a while. But then she found that she had too much time to think about reality. It made her nauseated to think of her husband's attempt to kill her. And the fact that she was no longer counted among the living. She missed her work, and her friend and co-worker, Claire. Margo began to cry and could not stop crying. She went for a walk and ended up finding a nice quiet place to contemplate her next move.

She walked for a while and ended up sitting on a large stone away from the cabin in a clearing near a grove of tall pine trees. Her dark blonde hair spread out over her shoulders, her skirt dragged on the ground as she sat there with her chin rested in her hands and leaning on her elbows in deep thought. Although the area was beautiful, and the cabin cozy and warm, Margo felt disoriented. She felt secure enough there but wondered how long this was going to go on. She realized at this point, she no longer existed according to law. She was dead and buried. She realized she needed to go to the authorities so she could get her life back in order. She missed her work especially her friend and co-worker, Claire. Margo arrived at the cabin in Sara's saucer so Margo had no idea where she was and she had no transportation to take her down the mountain. And where would she go? Where would she stay?

Margo was indeed feeling sorry for herself and she felt she had every right to be depressed. Her husband tried to kill her and that was the reality of it, like it or not. *Why was life so hard?* she wondered. *Where was the love?* All her life she had been tormented. Her father was cold. Growing up was very difficult as her father mistreated her. There were never any signs of affection from him. So as a young adult she was looking for a father like figure in a husband. She had dated several boys while in high school. They were handsome, tall, smart and had a lot of common sense, but she wasn't ready.

Several years out of high school she met her first husband James. He was older, divorced with two kids. They dated for a couple of years before they got married. They married after he got work in the factory and she worked as a secretary at the insurance company. After fifteen years James still had his job at the factory and Margo went from being a secretary to being a real estate agent. Marriage was not easy for them, they fought a lot about everything from his kids, why she never wanted any of her own, to money matters.

Margo's unconscious feelings of lack of control in her life turned inward and she developed health issues. She suffered through the years with ulcers and back pain. She felt trapped and only saw the future as more of the same of the past and felt very bleak about it.

James's two kids from his first marriage were young adults now and off on their own at college. They never really warmed up to her, as they spent most of their time with their mother, as James's ex-wife had custody while they were growing up. They were even more distant after James had his heart attack and died. So Margo mostly heard from them when they needed money, not the every other Sunday phone call home as they promised.

Margo wanted to get married but she found that she was a little afraid of marriage. Growing up Margo observed her parents arguing and physically fighting all the time. She saw her father was always the boss and got his way because as cultural norms had it, he was the head of the household and as the breadwinner, made more money than her. He was the main bread winner, and money was power.

Margo felt women were slighted. She saw her mother as a slave, like a secondary citizen. In those days, women fought over getting a good man and hanging on to him. Because it meant how the rest of your life was going to pan out. At an early age, along with baby dolls, girls were taught to love honor and obey her husband. Men possessed all the positions of authority. Boys were taught to be rough and tough to make good soldiers. People were told boys were good with numbers and should study math and economics, and girls only needed to study home economics. Girls were taught to be docile and trained to be like their mothers and love and obey their husbands, and the man should make all the decisions.

Growing up, Margo and other girls received a prayer books at their first communicant, then at their confirmation teaching them these things. So, just as girls went crazy over Elvis and the Beatles, Margo was James' constant fan and biggest cheer leader. She watched him play sports and was always there, sitting in the bleachers to cheer him on. She asked him to go bicycle riding with her; he promised but that never happened, he was too busy with sports. So she biked alone. She asked to see a particular movie, but that never happened either because he thought it was too much of a romantic girl's movie. She gave in, she had no choice. He couldn't be seen in a sissy girls' movie, so instead they saw the war movie he wanted to see. They only did the things that were his ideas.

But like most girls, even though she felt unhappy about it, she knew her place. She had been raised to be an adoring fan of her man, as was her mother to her father. She went shopping alone, rode her bicycle alone, and went to see the movies she wanted to see, alone. Sometimes, she wondered, why she was even married? Her girlfriends usually stayed at home and waited for their boyfriends or husbands to make plans for them, but Margo was getting tired of this and after Margo married James it did not take long before she soon found out that he only wanted to do the things he liked to do and would not do anything she liked to do.

He never helped her around the house or with his kids when they visited, that was women's work, he would protest. Men don't do women's work. When they went out with friends the women took the backseat to all conversations as the men were the entertainers and the authorities on every subject, even where women were concerned. Women listened. Men knew best. Margo hated facing the realities of this an authoritarian patriarchal society where males ruled and females were considered secondary citizens.

"Boys will be boys" she always heard and that it was up to the girl to say no and stop him before he went too far. Margo liked to blame authoritarian patriarchal religion for women's sorrowful fate. Men rule; therefore, men set to norms and the rules to please themselves. Margo grew to dislike authoritarian rule which was so prevalent throughout society. The man was boss, the woman was subservient, and men said Amen to that; of course, they loved it, they designed it that way. Why change anything as it was working for the men?

It was common social knowledge that if a girl got pregnant, it was her fault because boys cannot help themselves. Margo loathed this reality, yet there were no decent paying women's jobs for her to be able to strike out on her own. Women were paid less than men, so it was necessary for a young woman to get married, pregnant or not, to have a decent lifestyle and keep up with the Jones, as the saying goes. And once there were babies and kids there was no way she could ever leave the situation because the man made more money than a woman and she needed a roof over her head for herself and her kids.

James loved Margo more than she loved him, so she used fake kindness and affection to get what she wanted. She learned to cheer on her ideas he took credit for. It was the only way she would get him to do anything around the house or go anywhere with her. He definitely had to drive the car, so to speak, on every issue. She learned to play the game for her own survival, all women did although they hated to admit it. Many of her married friends felt that living with their husbands was like raising another child, but that was just the way it was. Everybody, all of their friends, liked James well enough and she figured that all men were cut from the same mold, so she readily married him. He had made a decent living, wasn't a drunk who drank up the paycheck on paydays, and he didn't beat her, so yes, he was good husband material.

Years later in 2020, Margo's thoughts would be solidified when she would read the book, *The End of Men*, by Hanna Rosin. The book satisfied her curiosity and suspicions that men as a whole seemed to be losing enthusiasm and taking a back seat staying home and babysitting the kids. What a turn of events. The book is about the last twenty or so years and how women have gained much ground and out-numbered men attending and graduating college and have entered once thought to be only men's careers. Seems women are doing it all. Women are beginning to outdo men in many professional careers. Margo was glad to read it because it confirmed her suspicions anyway. She also learned that the Anunnaki patriarchal rule of the Pisces Fourth Dimension was coming to an end. The year 2020 would bring the Pleiadian feminine rule of the Fifth Dimension's dawning of the Age of Aquarius. *Finally,* she thought.

Men had their thoughts about being the head of household, and many could not hold up the bargain. When Margo was first married to James, she soon discovered that James was depressed most of the time, because he was not very enthusiastic about having to work, period. James had trouble keeping a job. He worked best at being a used car salesman as he had the gift of gab, but sometimes a smart mouth if he thought he could not win over a potential buyer, to buy a vehicle. Potential buyers complained to management, and James never got along with his bosses, and he got fired. So he went from one dealership to another.

After a while, he began to drink a lot, the tavern became his second home. And after a time, he didn't even do that. He became more complacent, lazy and more of a recluse. She couldn't get him out of the house. He just sat watching television in his recliner all day while she was at work. In the morning when she left for work, he was in his chair; when she came home at night from work, he was still in his chair. He barely bathed and wore the same clothes day after day. He ate too much and was always stressed out when he had to go to work. He gained a lot of weight and his bad habits most likely brought on the heart attack that ended his life.

Margo was not surprised when he died. She knew that James ate and drank far too much, and Margo did not eat enough as she always took small portions as James got most of the food. James loved sweets. He always said he had a sweet tooth. By his request, Margo baked lots of rich pastries that were his favorites. She knew they were not good for him as he kept gaining weight. But, she just gave up on trying to save his sorry ass. She thought she would just keep him happy. Let him eat whatever he likes, as if she could stop him anyway, she thought.

After James died, Margo had his rather modest life insurance policy to help with his funeral and to help her out while she looked for a decent paying job. There were enough hairdressers in town, so Margo forgot about going to cosmetology school and instead decided on becoming a real estate agent. She studied hard and got her license and then went to work for a small man and wife owned real estate agency. Margo learned to just go along to be getting along. She was single for several years before she met Jack and she would have no problem being single again.

Chapter Twenty-Five

Sitting alone on the big stone in the clearing near the cabin, Margo had lots of time to think about the past and the future. She swore to herself that as soon as it was safe, she would contact her dear friend, Claire, and tell her that she was still amongst the living. She knew that the sooner she told her, the better. Having her think that she was dead and buried was the worse feeling she had ever had, and it depressed her. She felt totally out of her element. Margo felt ostracized from society. She somehow felt powerful and other worldly in a way. She wondered what she was going to do about Jack.

The burden was beginning to get her down and then she thought of Sara, her wonderful visual spirit guide. And being just a thought away, Sara suddenly appeared before her; a golden glow lit up the sky. Sara appeared before Margo as she sat on the big rock near her cabin, depressed, her head cast down fighting back the tears. She suddenly felt lifted, spiritual, and safe when Sara appeared before her. Sara appeared beautifully in a ray of light. Margo saw that Sara was practically transparent, surrounded by the bright light, and in a hooded robe-type gown. She looked more like an image of the Blessed Virgin than a Pleiadian Goddess from Alcyone, the most shining star of the Pleiades star system. Margo's eyes grew wide as she looked up at the woman in the light with a combination of excitement, fright, and astonishment. Sara in all her glory, glowed as she appeared. She appeared to be floating as her feet extended about twelve inches above the ground. Under her hood, her blonde hair surrounded her lovely face and dazzling clear green eyes. Margo looked up at her and cried.

"I think I am losing my mind," cried Margo, "I think I need your help."

"What can I do to help, my dear?" Sara asked looking down at the tearful pitiful woman sitting before her.

"Don't you think I need to go to the authorities and tell them who I am?"

"You could," Sara said softly as she tried to console Margo, who seemed to be at her wits end.

"Don't you think that I should?" asked Margo soundly sad.

"But, you don't know where Jack is, so let's wait just a bit, okay?" suggested Sara wanting to desperately help her friend but thinking they needed to come up with a plan first.

"Okay, but as of right now I no longer exist in the eyes of the law. I have no identification with me either. I would need someone to identify me. I don't know, will I need to get dental records? That is how they do it, isn't it, identify the deceased. My husband killed me, remember?"

"Yes, he ended your life as you have known it," explained Sara, "that's for sure."

"So I think I need to go to the police," stated Margo, "wouldn't you agree?"

"Well, let's think about how we are going to do this. In the meantime, we will keep you well supplied with whatever you need."

Margo agreed that she needed a little bit more time to think. She knew she could into get trouble holding out information to the authorities about her thoughts of her husband trying to kill her. She would just admit to loss of memory from hitting her head during the accident. Besides, she had no idea where, Jack, her murderer husband, was keeping himself. Margo wondered if he was still in town, or did he already take off the life insurance policy money? And Margo wondered about Joe. Joe knew that she was still alive, and that Jack killed and buried another woman in her place. In Margo's eyes, Joe was an accompaniment, an accessory, to Jack's crimes.

Sara had a tough time trying to convince Margo to be patient. She knew that she would have to quickly come up with a plan.

Chapter Twenty-Six

Jack and Judy were head over heels in love and hot romance. They were so in love in their whirlwind affair. As soon as Jack realized that Judy had lots of money, he decided he wanted to marry her as soon as possible. Oh, he treated Judy like a queen and easily won her over. Within two weeks after meeting, Jack hired a minister and had their run-away romance sealed in blissful matrimony. It was a small private ceremony at the same hotel outside bar where they met, complete with same bartender and waitress as their witnesses. They decided to stay and live in Florida. Judy, much to her grown children's concern and worry, had left them, friends, and relatives all behind in Memphis. She informed them that she was madly in love and beginning a new life with Jack, and they were going to live in Florida where they met.

Jack took out a two-million-dollar life insurance policy on her. He was greedy. He somehow convinced Judy to change her trust and will to exclude her children, because they protested the marriage. Jack was most pleased. Judy's two kids and their spouses had not been invited to the wedding because they protested the wedding. Selfishly, they had not wanted their mother sharing her money, their assumed inheritance, with her new husband. Jack was most happy with the new inheritance arrangement and madly in love with his new wife, Judy. She was a beautiful blonde-haired, blue-eyed beauty, who just happened to have lots of money.

Chapter Twenty-Seven

Jack wasn't the only wise one hiding his past and true identity, so was Judy. Unbeknownst to Jack, he had finally met his match. He had no idea that Judy's husband had a little help from her with having his heart attack. She had a huge life insurance policy on him. She was attracted to Jack and he to her, so easily caught him in her web. Jack was a ruggedly handsome guy with a great physique and brown wavy hair with a touch of gray at the temples. His good looks were his greatest assets. Her most significant asset was the two-million-dollar life insurance policy she took out on Jack. She had found that she could easily win him over and gain his trust and confidence, and he thought the same about her. They were both playing the same game.

Judy knew that Jack would be in for a rude awakening if he learned that Judy had dollar signs in her eyes when she first saw Jack. Judy was intrigued when she spotted him arriving alone at the hotel. Judy was at that bar for no other reason other than to meet Jack. And she knew that Jack would be attracted to her because she was pretty and wore expensive clothes. But more than that, the best thing was she was , sitting alone at the bar like pretty prey just wanting for the hungry hawk to swoop down, circle in and pounce on her. She suspected that she was monetary prey to Jack. She was very wise and intuitive. Of course she was, she was nobody's fool, and her plan was to get Jack's life insurance policy money before he got his hands on hers.

Chapter Twenty-Eight

Joe was excited about spending the evening with Claire and looked forward to their date. He could barely wait until she got off work at five. He was nervous and could not decide if he should wait outside or go in. He hee-hawed around about it for a moment pacing in front of her agency door when Claire appeared. His heart jumped, she was even prettier than he last remembered, and that was only hours earlier in the day.

"There you are, come in Joe, I want you to meet Mike and Sue who are the owners of the agency. Claire smiled at Joe's obvious nervousness. She could tell he was eager to meet her co-workers. The foursome stood and chitchatted about the business and the weather until Joe and Claire bid them farewell, and then smiled as Joe opened the door for Claire and as he followed her out, waved good-bye. It felt so natural to both of them as Joe took her hand and they strolled down the sidewalk toward the restaurant.

Foster City in the year 2020 was thriving, the suburbs were advancing into the fields where wheat, corn and soybeans were grown. Now houses were everywhere, it was a small and thriving Midwestern city. The downtown area was rather busy this time of the day with people getting off work and either heading home or sticking around and going out to dinner.

Foster City had a small history museum with glass cases and wooden shelves filled with historic tokens, equipment, books and pictures of the history of the coal mining and railroad that kept the town alive through the years. There were many craft, artsy shops and lots of small restaurants downtown near Claire's real estate office.

Claire loved a particular Italian restaurant that she frequented, and she knew Joe would love it too. They strolled arm in arm each silently appraising and admiring their reflections in the storefront picture windows. Their relationship being in the beginning stages posed questions for each of them, of course; but each secretly thought that they made a lovely couple as they admired their reflections in the large storefront windows. They chatted about her job and the nice couple who owned the realty business during their short walk to the restaurant. When they arrived, a young smiling hostess seated them at a small table in a cozy corner of the dining area. Before she left them, the hostess lit the candle stuck in the top wine bottle covered in wax that dripped down that sat centered on the red and white checkered tablecloth. Then she turned with a smile and went to get the bottle of wine they ordered.

"Isn't this lovely?" Claire's eyes sparkled, reflexing the candlelight that made her green eyes appear seductive and alluring.

"You are lovely," Joe murmured his happy heart all a flutter, "Here's to us." He raised his glass to hers in a toast.

"Here's to us," Claire repeated as they clinked their wine glasses together and proceeded to look over the menu. Both knew it was going to be a great dinner and a lovely evening.

Joe told Claire that he had decided he was going to get out more to socialize and enjoy life. He had been holding back since his wife died of foiled and toxic cancer treatments that apparently was rushed through FDA approval in order to get it on the market. Of course, the drug company pushed doctors to use it, and of course, insurance companies would not pay the coverage of the treatment. So Joe was left with mounting medical bills. He needed money badly. It had been nearly three years since his wife died.

He had sued the chemical company that made the knowingly toxic cancer treatment and pushed it through the FDA, which was overseen by a conservative senate that had appeased their largest campaign contributor by deregulating safety measures. He also sued the hospital and doctors that administrated the drugs, and so far nothing had come of it. The lawsuit was being held up in court in what was now becoming part of a class action lawsuit. Joe worked for an insurance company and he saw many similar claims each day. He saw that many health insurance claims were denied and this infuriated him. He had a ton of medical bills to pay for all the time his wife was sick and fighting for her life. Joe needed settlement money badly.

Joe in a way envied Jack's ability to get away with stuff. During the last few years Joe had watched his cousin and the mystery and intrigue that surrounded Jack's daring activities. Jack's mischievous adventures were beginning to rub off on Joe. He suspected his frustration and anger was allowing him to soak up some of Jack's evil ways. He could not help but admire Jack, even though he was still irritated with him for not paying him the money Jack owed him for getting his truck fixed. He was angry, but spending time with Claire had a way of getting him to forget these problems, if only temporarily.

Chapter Twenty-Nine

Joe had a wonderful evening with Claire. He was crazy about her and wanted to impress her. Dating this lovely woman was going to cost him money, money he did not have. Joe had to think of a way to get the money that Jack owed him. But where was Jack? The next day when he was at work at the broker insurance agency, he decided to look up Jack's life insurance policies he had carried. He found the one that paid out on Margo.

So decided to dig deeper into Jack's life insurance policies in the past and to his surprise he found that Jack had recently opened a life insurance policy on his new wife, Judy, with another life insurance company, different than the one he used for Margo. *Man this guy does not waste time,* Joe thought. Joe looked on and found that Jack's billing address was in Florida. Bingo! Joe thought.

He had a little vacation time coming, so he decided to make a trip to Florida to find Jack and get the money that Jack owed him for getting his truck fixed. He would have liked Claire to accompany him, but she had houses to show. He told her it was a business trip, and he would only be gone a couple of days. Claire wished she could have gone with him as she was feeling depressed missing her good friend, Margo, and getting away and would have helped taking her mind off of work.

Chapter Thirty

Claire had to blink back tears at work because each time she saw paperwork with Margo's name on it or heard her name mentioned by anyone she worked with, it brought her to tears. It was heartbreaking. Margo was always in the back of her mind, as if she could feel her presence around her. She missed her good friend and work partner. Going to work every day was just not the same without Margo, so she was glad that she had Joe in her life now to help fill the void. Many times, while with Joe she wanted to talk about Margo's sudden passing, but somehow the opportunity never really came up they were so busy talking about his work or about real estate, or the weather or what not. But mostly being with Joe the few times they had gone out just helped brighten her day.

Claire and Margo had been such good friends they had each other's back at work. Claire could always tell when Margo was in either physical or emotional pain, and she soon learned those events were associated with the way Jack was treating her at the time. Jack could be cold and cruel. One day when Claire first began working with Margo, Margo had come to work with a black eye. Margo swore she got it getting something out from below the counter and did not realize the cupboard door was open. She sported a black eye with a nasty scratch on her cheek. For a week or more she wore dark tinted glasses to try to hide it. But Claire saw it and into Margo's heart too, she knew Jack was the cause. And she knew Margo knew she knew, they just did not speak about it because it was too painful to talk about for either of them.

Claire realized Margo knew she should get away from Jack, it was just a matter of when. Margo was raised by a strict Catholic mother and like her mother, she felt that she had to honor her wedding vows and stick it out. Besides it was frightening to start over and begin again. Claire remembered though when she was at a luncheon with Margo and Margo mentioned something about seeing a lawyer and having divorce papers drawn up. But then it wasn't long after that on that rainy night that she ran off the road and had that horrible accident. Claire remembered hearing the news as if it were yesterday, and she cried as if she were being told all over again that her co-worker and friend was gone. *If only Margo was alive and she could talk to her,* she thought.

Chapter Thirty-One

"Sara, are you there?" asked Margo. She knew Sara was just a thought away. Margo was sitting on that big rock again in the clearing away from the cabin. She had to get outdoors in the daylight and recharge her emotional batteries, as she was feeling poorly.

"You called, my dear," Sara said suddenly appearing in mid-air about a foot off the ground. She was, as before, all aglow in the same hooded robe garment. In the bright light, she appeared like the Blessed Virgin Mary had come to visit her.

"I'm getting cabin fever, if you don't mind the pun," Margo replied. She couldn't resist the pun, after all she was living in a cabin.

"I'll see what I can do for you," Sara knew she had to help Margo. Sara also knew things were heating up in regard to Jack now that Judy was in the picture and Joe was heading to Florida. Sara could only observe events and usually was not to interfere in the process.

"Please hurry," begged Margo.

"Want to have a little fun?" asked Sara smiling.

"Sure," Margo said.

"How about a trip to Florida?" asked Sara.

"Sure, I would love it," agreed Margo.

"How about a first-class ticket in a spacecraft?"

"I'm packed and ready."

"Great," Sara was happy that Margo was happy.

"But why Florida?" asked Margo.

"It's where Jack and his new wife are living."

"Holy crap."

Margo knew all too well what Jack's true colors were and what evil he was capable of doing. He was a bad guy, and Margo was more than willing to do anything to help another one of Jack's potential victims escape his deadly grasp.

"Hurry now, get your things," encouraged Sara, "I will wait for you here."

Chapter Thirty-Two

Joe took a cab from the airport and checked in a hotel close to the address he found on Jack's new life insurance policy application he submitted. He walked around the complex and sat on the crowded patio every day in hopes of seeing Jack in the crowd. He watched and waited, and the next day he spotted Jack strolling through the shops and restaurant area with an attractive woman. They both were sharply dressed and made an impressive looking couple. Jack had a new classic, rich appearance about him. It was apparent to Joe that Jack's new wife was evidently picking out his clothes and dressing him, as they looked as if they both stepped out of a fashion magazine.

Joe watched the happy couple as they strolled along holding hands. They walked up to a spa entrance in the adjacent mall where he kissed her on the cheek and she went in. Joe had followed far enough behind as not to be seen. He watched as Jack walked over to a cafe where he ordered a brew and newspaper and sat at a table in the sunshine. This was Joe's opportunity to walk over and speak to Jack while he was sitting there alone. So he slowly walked up to the table where Jack was sitting and slipped into one of the chairs at the table.

"Hello Jack," Joe quietly said and then took pleasure in watching Jack look up at him as if he saw a ghost.

"What the?" Jack said, startled as he looked up to see a familiar face he did not want to see. His breath was caught in his throat for a second as his heart beat shot into overdrive.

"How you doing, Jack?" Joe asked with an evil tone to his voice.

"What are you doing here?"

"I came to get my share of the money," snarled Joe, "certainly looks like you could spare the money." Joe looked Jack up and down as he said it. "Looks like you have done very well for yourself."

"What money?" asked Jack with a startled look on his face.

"The money you owe me for getting your truck fixed after you messed it up when you ran your wife off the road," Joe rose his voice in anger.

"What?" Jack shot back in an angry tone.

"You heard me," confirmed Joe.

"Hey, lower your voice, will you," demanded Jack and went on to clear the air.

"I will not," snapped back Joe.

"I did not run her off the road. She must have lost control. I told you I messed up my truck when I sideswiped that pole."

"Never mind that, just give me the money you owe me, remember I used my money to get your truck fixed," snarled Joe angrily.

"Okay, okay, I'll get you your money," Jack shot back, "jeez."

"I expect the cash by tomorrow," demanded Joe.

"That's impossible," declared Jack.

"Tomorrow, or I tell your latest lovely wife what you are really like," Joe said moving up close across the table and getting into Jack's face.

"Tomorrow is impossible," repeated Jack.

"Tomorrow," Joe demanded. "I'll be at this table tomorrow afternoon at two, be here with the money, or I'll share your shady past with your new wife."

"You can't do that," demanded Jack.

"Oh, yes I can," said Joe with confidence. Joe was shaking inside but feeling strong and powerful. He had Jack over a barrel. Jack had to comply. Joe looked Jack over as he got up from the table thinking soon he would wear fancy clothes.

Jack was appalled. He sat frozen for a few minutes trying to figure out what he was going to do. Yes, he could pay off Joe, give him the money he promised. He guessed he should have done that in the first place, but he got caught up in the excitement of the moment and got greedy. He figured Joe would be no threat. He was wrong. Joe could easily turn him in to the insurance company and the law. He was going to have to deal with Joe very soon, but how? He wanted to concentrate on his new life with his new wife. He thought he would put Joe off for a while by just giving him the money he expected. After all, he did promise the money to Joe. But Jack was leery about Joe's loyalty.

Jack did not trust Joe. Joe was acting weird as if he had something to hide; something to use against him. Jack was becoming uneasy. Now he had loose ends. Loose ends that could really mess up his new life with his new wealthy bride who adored him. His new situation was perfect. She was fun. She had money and they had talked about making plans to travel the world. But now Joe was going to be in the picture. Sooner or later Joe was going to have to be dealt with. Jack looked at his watch and saw his wife was about to be finished at the spa, so he got up and walked over there. He got to the spa entrance as she was coming out of the door.

"Hi babe," smiled Jack, "you look amazing." She did look fantastic, he wanted to show her off.

"Why, thank you darling," Judy smiled and kissed Jack on the cheek.

"How about dinner at that restaurant and you said the other day you would like to try?" Jack said.

"That sounds wonderful, being pampered at the spa has given me an appetite," laughed Judy. Judy was enjoying herself watching this man fall all over her. He was amusing, kind and gentle and handsome. She admired their reflections in the store front windows as they strolled the avenue. They made a perfectly lovely couple. The kind of guy any woman would want to show off. She actually thought she might miss him when this particular episode of her life was over.

Chapter Thirty-Three

The next afternoon, Jack made an excuse to get coffee from the nearby Starbucks. He asked Judy if she wanted him to bring her back something. She was sitting on their patio in her bathing suit soaking up the sun and reading a book. The day was warming and she was getting hot and thirsty, so requested he bring back an iced chai latte. He readily agreed. He quickly kissed her on the cheek and departed, as it was close to two o'clock and time to meet up with Joe.

Jack had the cash in an envelope. He had gotten up early and made an off-shore bank wire-transfer the money to a local bank. The clerk at the bank did not bat an eye as they lived in a wealthy Palm Beach area where very large wire transfers were done all the time. Jack was glad and just wanted to get the transaction done and Joe off his back.

As he walked to the coffeeshop he spotted Joe sitting at the designated table where they had planned to meet. Jack saw Joe smile when he saw Jack was carry an over-stuffed envelope.

"Have a seat, please," Joe said pulling out a chair for Jack. He was all smiles and feeling good about getting his hands on lots of money.

"Here's your damn money," Jack said in a low voice as he threw the envelope on the table and flopped himself down in a chair.

"Great," Joe said as he reached for the envelope and peeked inside.

"Sure cost enough to get my truck fixed," complained Jack.

"Well, you know that blue paint from Margo's blue car all over the side of your black truck was hard to get off according to the collision technician. He took pictures before and after he was so proud of his work. See he sent me copies," sported Joe with blackmail pride. He had ammo, full-colored photos, just in case he ever needed it.

"Hey what are you driving at?" Jack demanded to know.

"Well, maybe you can easily impress women, but ' I'm on to you Jack," Joe was mad and almost hinted that Margo was alive. But Joe did not know where Margo was, she had disappeared. Joe was even beginning to question his own sanity, since he saw Margo only the day of her funeral at her house on her couch. Joe had not seen Margo since her funeral. He wished he had taken a selfie of him and her to have as proof. Maybe he was going crazy. Maybe he only thought he saw her. Joe decided not to mention anything about Margo being alive, although he would have loved to have seen Jack squirm in fear just a bit.

Chapter Thirty-Four

Margo loved the cabin, but time passed by there very slowly. So she was very happy to be going away with Sara. A change would do her good. She had spent her time reading and painting pictures of the beautiful surrounding pine tree mountainous scenery. She cooked, she cleaned, she read nearly all the books on the wooden shelves that bordered the fireplace in the den. She had been feeling isolated, so was glad to be leaving. In minutes Margo was back where Sara was waiting for her.

"Are you ready to go?" asked Sara.

"You bet I am," Margo replied with a happy tone. She was ready for a change, she was lonely, and she was bored. She was the victim so why should her life suddenly have to stop while Jack was free to do whatever he wanted.

"I know you are sad," revealed Sara.

"You bet I am," Margo complained. "Why am I hiding while Jack gets to do whatever he wants, and has lots of money to do it with. It's not fair."

"I agree," sympathized Sara, "and we are going to do something about it."

"Like what?" asked Margo in a tone sounding like a desperate plea.

"Want to go for a ride?" she said in the same way the scientist said to Jodie Foster's character in the movie "Contact."

"Sure," smiled Margo, "can I drive?"

Wasn't long and they were airborne in Sara's silver saucer with Margo at the helm.

"Oh this is so cool," Margo said maneuvering the craft to and fro, up and down and sideways.

"My dear, just because I am a Pleiadian does not mean I am beyond getting motion sickness," Sara said with a grimace, "could you please take it easy?"

"Sure, okay," Margo said, "sorry." But most of her attention was in guiding the spacecraft.

"Now that I have practiced my maneuvers, just where are we headed?" asked Margo.

"Florida," commanded Sara, "concentrate on Palm Beach, Florida."

"Okay Palm Beach it is." Margo did not care where they went, as long as she could command the craft.

"Why Florida," Margo finally asked, "any particular reason?"

"Why yes, my dear," stated Sara, "we are going to give Jack a visit."

"What," exclaimed Margo, "you know where he is?"

"Oh yes."

"Really," exclaimed Margo, "Well, can this bucket of

bolts go any faster?" Margo laughed at the strange look on Sara's face.

"Laugh's on you, my dear," frowned Sara, "because as it is we are there already."

"Wow!" Margo was speechless.

"Margo, think Beach Front Luxury Hotel," ordered Sara, "that will take us right to him.

"How do you know that?" asked Margo.

I'll let you in on a secret. Our thoughts create our realities. Our consciousness and our thoughts are universal. So, just a thought away. We only have to know how to tap into another's consciousness and thoughts to find out what they are up to."

"You are kidding me, right?" asked Margo.

"No, my dear, I kid you not," smiled Sara. It's true; this universe is one big consciousness; all are consciously alive and regular as a heartbeat. One only has to learn how to tap into another's field of consciousness. It's how psychic mediums connect with passed loved ones. When we die only our physical body dies, our consciousness, our souls, live on."

"Well, okay then," sighed Margo feeling excited in a strange way. *What a ride*, she thought. Indeed! Everything up to the present since her unlikely and untimely death has been magical!

Sara took command of the craft's controls over Palm Beach, and positioned them above cirrostratus cumulous clouds, which she created using magnified radar sonar technology. As they hovered, hidden from sight, above the clouds over the Beach Front Luxury

Hotel, they cruised at a reasonably low altitude. Within a few seconds, they spotted Jack and Judy on the craft's radar zoom screen.

"On my," exclaimed Margo, "That is Jack sitting on that lounging chair."

"Yes, it is," Sara agreed.

"Who is that woman with him?"

"Brace yourself," warned Sara.

"Why?" asked Margo.

"That woman is, Judy, his new wife."

"Holly crap, he is married again already?" exclaimed Margo.

"Afraid so," replied Sara.

"Unbelievable," exclaimed Margo, "all of this is unbelievable. Am I dreaming? Maybe I did die, and I just do not realize that I am dead?"

"You are alive, my dear," smiled Sara, "trust me, you are very alive."

It took Margo a few minutes to collect herself. The whole experience felt so other-worldly, which of course it was. She felt otherworldly too, but then suddenly, very human emotions rose from the depths of her soul: jealously, anger, and most of all, the desire for revenge.

"This is so exciting," said Margo with a wicked smile, "you have really turned my life around." She thought for a second, then added, "wait, you saw the movie "Contact" in a theatre on Alcyone?"

"No, my dear, I watched it with you long ago when the movie first came out. I was sitting there next to you, in spirit."

"I love that, wow, just a thought away and I didn't even know it," Margo said feeling touched.

Chapter Thirty-Five

Judy and Jack had wasted no time getting married, both saying they were not getting any younger and would be foolish to play the waiting game. Judy loved being married to Jack, for she had a plan in place and a life insurance policy on Jack., Of course, Jack did not know that. She loved him in her own selfish way. He was tall, dark, and handsome, and she looked good on his arm as their reflections in the shop windows confirmed. Arm in arm, they strolled down the streets and shopped at all the high fashion tourist shops. They looked good and they were living the good life in Palm Beach, going to plays, movies, dances, concerts, and taking dinner cruises, just enjoying life. Judy had buried her previous husband only within the past two years. Things were going right for her now, and she honestly hoped to hang onto Jack for a while, well, until her money ran low.

Chapter Thirty-Six

Sara and Margo spied on Jack and Judy from Sara's silver saucer as it hovered over the hotel, shapeshifting to appear as light stratus cumulus wispy clouds so they would not be detected from the ground.

"Look at him sitting there in all his narcissistic glory," groaned Margo.

"He does appear to be enjoying himself," claimed Sara.

"She too!" griped Margo, "But what can we do?"

"Let's just watch them for a bit," suggested Sara.

The two sat there and pondered their choices. Margo was feeling protective of Jack's wife but revengeful as far as Jack was concerned. She thought she could just walk up to him and say hello, that should be enough to freak him out. Then she could just tell his new wife exactly what Jack did to her. She could describe in detail how Jack deliberately forced her off the road, leaving her to die in the cold, murky floodwaters. But Margo wasn't really feeling it this day, the ride to where she was sitting right now was just too spectacular and magical.

Chapter Thirty-Seven

Joe returned from his trip to Florida several thousand dollars richer. He and Claire enjoyed a wonderful dinner at their favorite restaurant to celebrate. Joe toasted Claire upon the news of receiving her award for selling the most expensive houses in the area. Her record now was second to Margo's record. Her accomplishments and rewards were bittersweet. Margo had taught her well. She missed Margo and was sad receiving the recognition without her friend beside her. Joe thought Claire was doing wonderfully well and he was proud of her accomplishments and bonuses.

Joe was moving to a higher position at the insurance company where he worked and now was a manager overseeing twenty-four agents who reported to him. Joe was becoming very successful but along with his success he was becoming more and more greedy. Joe was competitive, and the idea that Jack was gaining millions from life insurance policies was eating at him.

He wanted in on the gig and planned to asked Claire to marry him. He wanted to elope right away.

"You are looking rather sad for an award winner, Claire," sighed Joe.

"Well, I was just missing Margo," she blurted out, fighting back tears.

"You know you didn't get to go to Florida with me because you were so busy selling all those homes. How about we go now for a few days to celebrate your big achievement award?"

"Why, that would be wonderful," Claire murmured as she kissed him.

"Well, if it gets me more of those sweet kisses, let's leave tomorrow."

"I took a few days off to celebrate, so that would be perfect," Claire was eager for a break and some Florida sun."

"Shall we pack a few things and leave tomorrow, then?" asked Joe.

"Tomorrow is perfect," Claire laughed with delight, "I love spontaneity. "

They began packing, and Joe called the hotel where he had stayed in Florida. Joe was in love and felt so hopeful that he arranged for a minister to marry them when they arrived. Jack and Judy could be witnesses. Joe was excited about his plan to marry Claire.

"Will you marry me?" Joe kissed Claire glad to hear that she loved spontaneity,

"Yes," Claire answered through tears. It felt right. She was thrilled to be getting married. She would have loved Margo to be her maid of honor, but having Judy and Jack as witnesses would be fine. She was ready to begin a new life with Joe.

By late afternoon on the following day, they met Jack and Judy at the hotel chapel and were married. Joe carried Claire over the threshold of their hotel room then they kissed their way to the bedroom. They were married. The ceremony had been small but lovely. The hotel decorated and provided a string quartet. The ceremony was short, sweet, and to the point. Joe treated the foursome to Dom Perignon champagne and prime rib dinner at a five star restaurant. They enjoyed themselves. Judy and Claire hit it off, and Jack and Joe had mended their fences, so all was good.

Back at their hotel suite, they headed right into the bedroom.

"I love you and I love this suite," Claire said as she kissed Joe. "It's so beautiful. And we can open the balcony doors and hear and see the ocean from here. This is wonderful. Thank you darling. What a wonderful idea you had."

"Only the best for my beautiful and talented super-selling real estate agent bride."

"I love it, and I love you." This was the happiest day of her life.

Joe and Claire spent the night making love then falling to sleep in each other's arms. They stayed in all day the next day and ordered a late breakfast. And made love all afternoon.

"I love you," Joe kissed her long and sweet. "Are you getting hungry? I sure am."

"Yes, I am. My gosh its almost four already, no wonder I am feeling hungry."

"What are you hungry for?" asked Joe kissing her and gently patting her belly.

"Well at this point I could eat anything." Judy pointed out, "You were here before, do you have any favorite restaurants?"

"Why yes, I do. There is a great Italian restaurant not far from here and it might be even better than our favorite Italian restaurant around the corner from your real estate office," suggested Joe and they headed in to take a quick shower and get dressed. It only took them a few minutes.

"Ready?" asked Joe.

"Yes, I am," smiled Claire, as she grabbed their jackets and he led the way to the door. They laughed and walked arm in arm out of the hotel lobby onto the sidewalk. It was a beautiful evening. Jack and Judy were to meet them at the restaurant.

Chapter Thirty-Eight

It was early evening, and Sara and Margo were heading out for dinner. Sara and Margo saw Jack and Judy walking out of the hotel from another exist as they walked out.

"That guy looks like Jack," exclaimed Margo.

"Why yes, I do believe that is Jack," Sara agreed.

"And that woman must be Judy, his new wife. So much for mourning me, Jack. I haven't been dead that long."

"I guess we all mourn in different ways, my dear," Sara said with a slightly sarcastic tone.

"You know I could really work this dead thing couldn't I?" joked Margo. Her mind was racing. Being dead, and no longer existing--she was thinking of ways she could use this to her advantage.

When Sara and Margo got to the nearby restaurant it appeared to be pretty crowded, but they saw a few people sitting outside on the patio having a drink as they waited for a table to open up.

"Look at all the people," exclaimed Margo, "the food must be good here."

"Let's get a drink on the patio; I see open tables."

Sara and Margo cozied up to the bar and were waited on right away. They ordered gin and tonic and as they turned to head to the patio, they saw that Jack and Judy sitting at a table with another couple; Margo did not recognize them at first. Then Margo suddenly realized who they were.

"Holy crap, that's Joe and my best friend, Claire," Margo could barely contain herself. She wanted to run into Claire's arms. "My gosh, she looks good, and she is with Jack's cousin, Joe. I had no idea they even knew each other. They look pretty cozy."

"It's beginning to seem like old home week," noted Sara, "as if she had no clue that this scenario was about to happen."

"Yes, a reunion of sorts," laughed Margo, "should we crash it?"

"We could," Sara responded cautiously.

"I'm not worried about Jack, and Joe knows, but I am worried about shocking Claire to death when she sees that I am alive," Margo sounded worried.

"You have a point there," said Sara, "and I wonder if the shock would be too much for her."

"I'll have to get her off to the side," sighed Margo, "to tell her it's me. I am not dead,"

"Well, it appears that the foursome is having a good time," observed Sara as they watched from a cafe table hidden behind tall plants.

"Oh my gosh," whispered Margo, "she's with Joe?" Margo was in shock. It took all of her emotional strength not to rush over to where Claire was sitting. Sara placed her hand on Margo arm and slightly shook her head not to.

"I would love to get Claire off to the side so I can talk to her," Margo wanted to cry and run into Claire's arms at the sight of seeing her. She missed Claire so much. What was she to do? She was tired of waiting and hiding out all alone while Jack lived the good life with a new wife. *She was the victim here. Why was she the victim in hiding,* she wondered.

In a way Claire help put up a shield between Margo and Jack. Because if Claire wasn't sitting there Margo would have been over there in Jack's face with the police right behind her. But seeing Jack, Margo had to admit to herself that there was something terribly wrong with Jack's psychic. Sara and Margo watched Jack, Judy, Joe and Claire sitting and chatting with one another.

The foursome looked like they had a nice dinner; anyway, it included four bottles of wine, so they should have not been feeling any pain. They huddled together and Margo figured they were making plans of some sort. She overheard them asking the waiter if he could recommend snorkeling outfitters. They were making plans to go snorkeling the next day. It wasn't long after that the foursome left the restaurant, Sara and Margo following not far behind. That night, Margo couldn't fall asleep, but when she finally did, she dreamed of Claire.

Chapter Thirty-Nine

They enjoyed beautiful sunny skies the next morning as the foursome, Jack and Judy, and Joe and Claire, got on the boat that took them out to the coral reefs where they could swim around and explore the colorful beauty of the clear turquoise waters. Snorkeling was a new experience for all four of them. They were so excited and loved seeing the colorful coral and the amazing colorful fish that swam to and fro and close by. The fish seemed curious and just as excited to see the humans as the humans were excited to see them. Each couple went their own way exploring and soon were separated.

Jack was feeling his old sinister self and couldn't help but take advantage of the opportunity that presented itself. He swam with Judy who smiled as she pointed out an area of huge coral reefs and beautiful colorful fish. Jack saw the warning sign posted near the water. It was a warning for tourist not to venture out too far and to be careful the coral was big and rough with sharp edges.

Jack saw the signs but instead of warning Judy, he urged her on ignoring the warning sign as he steered her into the forbidden area. As soon as they entered the forbidden area, a sudden surge of underwater current knocked Judy off balance and threw her violently against the coral reef. The current forced her leg to get caught in the coral. She struggled and the top air intake of her snorkel equipment got tangled in algae vines. The more she struggled and panicked, the more she became twisted and tangled. Jack tried to free her or at least pretended he was trying to free her.

Judy struggled fiercely to no avail. It seemed the more she struggled the more entangled she became. Jack saw she might get herself free while pretending to help her, only to twist her further around in the vines. She struggled and Jack saw blood rising from her trapped leg. Her eyes grew large behind her goggles as he pulled the vines which drug her further down where the air intake of her snorkel was now submerged. She fought to swim up while trying to untangle herself. Her eyes pleaded for help as Jack easily distanced himself further away from her, as to not get tangled up himself.

He watched as the air and life itself was snuffed out of her. He did not see death, rather his greedy heart saw dollar signs. Quickly he circled around and around looking for Joe and Claire. He rose to the surface and spotted their snorkels sticking up above the waves. He yelled for help and swam over to them. When Claire and Joe heard Jack holler they swam over to him. He was screaming and crying when they reached him, yelling Judy's name.

"What happened?" asked Joe.

"I found Judy all tangled up, I tried to untangle her," cried Jack but it was too late. Jack led Joe and Claire to where Judy was floating lifelessly several feet below the surface of the water still tethered to the coral reef by the vines. It was a horrendous sight. Joe and Claire were in shock as Jack tried his hardest to appear shocked also.

Joe saw the boat that took them out there off in the distance and signaled it to come to them. When it got closer, he reported what had happened to Judy. The captain called the coast guard rescue crew to untangle and recover Judy's body.

Chapter Forty

"Okay, I think I have the plan that should work," Sara knew it was time to dish the dirt on Jack and free up Margo so she could go back to being herself. Sara realized too that according to their laws, Margo could be in trouble for not coming forth with the truth much sooner. She knew the authorities would ask why Margo waited until after her funeral to come forth and expose her husband, Jack. *Amnesia,* she thought. *Margo could play the amnesia card if she had to.*

"Good, I am glad it is time to expose Jack," replied Margo. "I am ready to expose the truth about Jack. He should be arrested for the murderer that he is. He thought he killed me. When he couldn't find my body, he killed a woman to replace my body for the purpose of having one for the funeral and to collect the life insurance policy money."

Margo was getting more and more restless and so Sara decided to put a plan into place.

"Okay, Jack and Judy usually get breakfast at the

diner next door to where they live. Let's just be there too, and see how he takes to seeing you, Margo. We'll do something subtle like a walk by, or we can sit several tables away from them in clear view for Jack to see you."

Sara and Margo visited the cafe several mornings in a row, but Jack and Judy never showed up. Then finally one morning Jack walked up to the diner alone and sat at a small table on the perimeter of the patio,

"There he is," whispered Sara, "this is perfect."

"I'm a bit nervous. Should we be in public to do this, what if he throws some kind of horrendous fit?."

"He can't because it would expose to the world what a lying murderer he truly is," warned Sara.

"Okay then let's go in,"

"Table for two," the hostess asked.

"Yes, please, on the patio if there is a table available."

"Yes, I believe there is, follow me please," said the young pretty hostess with a pleasant voice.

Sara followed the hostess and Margo trailed behind feeling slightly nervous to confront her husband. But then thought, *why should I feel nervous? He is the one who will be nervous when he sees the wife he thought was long dead come walking in.*

"How is this table?" asked the hostess.

"Oh, this is perfect," answered Sara as she picked the side of the table with her back to Jack so Margo could sit opposite and face Jack who sat reading the paper and sipping a mug of coffee.

"I feel like a conspicuous fool for some reason," whispered Margo to Sara as she stole glances around

Sara's head to see Jack's face. But then seeing Jack sitting there alone looking rather pathetic changed her mind. She was better than this. Since Margo had met Sara and realized her super cool Pleiadian Hybrid origin, Jack was like a mere speck of lint on black slacks to her, just simply annoying. She pushed her nervousness to the side and allowed the good old-fashioned healthy sense of anger to emerge. Jack did not notice her. Within a few minutes, Margo saw Joe and Claire walked out onto the patio to join Jack at his table.

"My god, it's Joe and Claire," sighed Margo. Her heart ached when she spotted Claire.

Joe and Claire headed right for Jack's table without looking around, so they did not see Margo. Claire sat next to Jack and was also facing Margo's direction. They were several tables apart on the crowded patio.

"Oh, holly crap," exclaimed Margo.

"What?" asked Sara.

"Joe and Claire just came in and sat down at Jack's table," reported Margo as she ducked behind Sara a bit, not be spotted by the threesome across the way. She wasn't ready for Joe and Claire to see her, much less Jack. She needed to build up her nerve a bit more first.

"Oh boy, the plot thickens."

"May I take your order please," asked the young waitress, and Sara and Margo both jumped in their seats. They had been concentrating so hard on the table across the way that the waitress startled them.

"I'll have coffee and a cheese danish," answered Sara in response.

"I'll have the same," replied Margo, she was too shook to even think about looking through the menu.

"You know sooner or later either Jack, Joe, or Claire will recognize me, or certainly think that I remind them of someone." Margo knew that it had not been that long and that she indeed looked the same, nothing had really changed about her appearance, except maybe her hair was a bit longer.

Chapter Forty-One

Joe was a happy go lucky guy and Claire was the sweet, polite and silent type who really did not talk much unless someone asked her about her job. Then, Claire could talk anyone's ear off about the real estate business which she had grown to love. Slowly and surely she was beginning to overcome her grief for Margo. She still missed her, but her sadness was becoming more manageable. She knew she just had to go on living, breathing and working without her best friend, Margo, no matter how sad it made her.

Claire fell silent thinking of Margo as she listened to pitiful Jack mourn the death of Judy. The funeral had been swift, sad, and brief as Judy's adult children, did not attend, but wanted the urn with her ashes, so the ashes were divided between them. Joe was quiet having attended another funeral of one of Jack's wives, his second in under two years. Joe was becoming very suspicious of Jack and knew that he should turn Jack in, but Joe knew there was no proof of wrongdoing in either Judy or Margo's death. *Well, not until Margo decides to show herself*, he thought.

Margo observed the threesome across the way. She desperately wanted to get Claire off to the side. So keeping her head down to not be recognized, she sent the waitress over to discreetly whisper to Claire that she was needed inside. Joe and Jack were knee deep in baseball talk, and they barely noticed when Claire got up.

"I'm going to the restroom," whispered Claire to Joe and he nodded in return as she got up and walked inside the building. She headed to the restroom as she was instructed by the waitress. In the restroom Margo nervously awaited Claire's entrance. Margo was glad she was alone in the restroom when she heard the door open and saw Claire walk in.

"Please don't freak out Claire," whispered Margo, removing her big flopping hat and sunglasses, "it's me." Claire did not know what to expect, she was ready to catch Claire should she look like she would faint. As it was, Claire's eyes grew very large, and for a moment she couldn't speak as tears rose up in her eyes.

"What the hell?" whispered Claire as she rushed to Margo to touch her and make sure she was real, "damn it, I knew deep down that you were not dead, I just knew it, I felt it." She grabbed and held onto Margo tightly and they both quietly cried in each other's arms.

"Damn I missed you," cried Claire, "I needed you."

"I wanted to tell you so badly, but I couldn't," explained Margo and she quickly went on to tell Claire how her car ended up in the water, and how Jack had to have killed that woman who got buried at the funeral meant for her. She quickly mentioned Sara's silver saucer in passing.

"What silver saucer?" asked Claire with a puzzled look. She was about as surprised as she could get and had reached her surprise limit for one day. Margo knew to go easy on her but couldn't resist, she just had to share.

"Oh, by the way, another shock," whispered Margo in a hurried voice, "I'm here with Sara she is a Pleiadian who saved my life and has been helping me. I'll tell you more about her later. You'll like her because she is heavenly and magical."

"Whatever you say," moaned Claire as if to say what else could be more strange than your dead friend appearing in the restroom when you are out for breakfast.

Sara planned to share more detail about magical Sara later. She did not want to keep Claire from her table much longer. Just then the waitress stuck her head in the restroom door and said that a guy name Joe was asking if she was okay. So Claire nodded, quickly dried her eyes, kissed Margo then headed back to her table to rejoin Joe and Jack. As she desperately tried to act as if nothing as earth shattering as seeing the dead had just happened. And to make it worse, knowing you were sharing your breakfast table with the man who tried to kill her. And then the theatrics began, as planned out in the restroom by Margo and Claire. Right on cue when Claire got back to the table and sat down next to Jack and Joe, she pretended she spotted Margo across the patio at another table, or her "lookalike."

Claire pretended that she spotted a Margo's "look alike" at a table across the way. Suddenly she was speechless and her mouth dropped open, and she had to stop eating her bacon and eggs and stare at the loving woman across the way from her. Sara moved her head ever so slightly that Claire had a full view of Margo's face. Margo could feel Claire's eyes on her, eyes of recognition. When Margo stole a glance back at them, she could see the look of shock and disbelief rise on Claire's face. *Good plan Claire, she deserves an award,* she thought.

"Oh, oh. I believe Claire is doing a great job pretending to begin to recognize me," Margo spoke barely above a whisper and Sara leaned closer in to catch what Margo had to say.

"Honey, you look like you are about to begin to cry," observed Sara.

"She's my best friend," whispered Margo, "and I have really missed her more than I have realized. I want to run to her and hug her all over again."

"What is Jack doing?" asked Sara, facing Margo and not daring to turn around to see for herself.

"Mostly talking with Joe and glancing up every once in a while to look around."

"I think it is time we make some noise so they all look this way," announced Sara.

And before Margo had a second to protest and argue that point, Sara knocked her porcelain coffee cup saucer onto the brick patio floor and it loudly chattered into a million pieces that flew all over.

"Oh crap," declared Sara.

"No shit," Margo was shocked. She knew now that all hell was about to break lose.

The waitress came rushing over to pick up the pieces as now Jack, Claire, and Joe raised their heads to look around to see just what caused the noise. Jack suddenly got a stricken look on his face which turned bright red; then in seconds it seemed all the color drained from his face and he became ghostly white. Margo happily observed his discomfort. *How fitting,* she thought, *he looks as if he has just seen a ghost.* Margo got all excited about the dreadful appearance on Jack's face. *He deserved to feel shocked. He deserved to suffer a bit,* she thought.

Margo felt very brave now, and just as the waitress turned to leave with a dustpan of broken porcelain pieces, Margo jumped up and walked over to Claire. Claire was so glad that she knew beforehand what was going to happen as they had planned it out while they met in the restroom a few minutes earlier. Claire seeing Margo's pretty green eyes, smiled and prepared herself to act shocked. The moment caught up with her though, and she almost did feel like fainting, but kept her cool for she did not want to miss the chance of looking into her best friends eyes, and the chance to hold her close to her heart.

"Claire."

"Margo."

Claire and Margo rushed to each other and embraced.

"It's okay, do not pass out on me," whispered Margo.

"What the hell happened," cried Claire loudly holding Margo, "I went to your funeral."

"Well, you went to someone's funeral, it was not mine," declared Margo, "you'll have to ask my widower husband, Jack, for details as to who got buried that day.

Jack looked suddenly shocked as Margo, Claire and Joe all stared at him. Sara observed from a few feet away and had the waitress call the police and ask for a detective Johnson who she had been confiding in.

Joe and Jack both turned and stared at Margo standing there in Claire's arms.

"Oh oh," was all Joe could say. In the time Joe was dating Claire, he had not even hinted to Claire that Margo could possibility still be alive. He only said something about the closed casket due to being in the elements for so long. He would say to Claire when she cried in his arms missing Margo , that there were several people reported missing by police and feared to have possibly drowned in the fast rising flood waters.

Claire looked on with surprise at the freakish expression on Jack's face. According to Joe's summation, Jack looked like a man who had seen a ghost, a real ghost, as if his conscious was getting the better of him. Joe appeared to be the most collected and comfortable, since he knew Margo had indeed survived the car accident, as he had seen her at her house on the day of her funeral. He was glad that he chose not to tell Jack that Margo was still alive because the look now on Jack's face was priceless.

"What?" Jack's eyes were wide open in shock as he sprung up from the chair at the sight of Margo. One word was all he could utter above a whisper as he turned and saw Margo looking healthy and alive walking towards him. He felt like fainting and had to sit back down quickly. Jack looked like the kid who got caught red-handed with his hand in the cookie jar. For a second he felt confused and dumbfounded and knew his run of fast love and money was over. Sooner or later, if not the law, the insurance companies would have caught on as Joe had been investigating suspicions brought forth by record clerks who worked with him.

Joe only smiled and Margo smiled back at him and nodded. Jack sat speechless with coffee dripping from his twisted sagging bottom lip as if he had had a stroke. He began to mumble some unrecognizable sounds. His large eyes fixed on Margo as if he was seeing a ghost or merely the hint of his own demise. He knew he was in serious trouble.

"So, Jack, just who did you bury in my name?" asked Margo. She was upset and livid and now that she had Jack cornered the words just came out. She could not resist taunting him about what he had done to her and other women before her. The audacity to think that he thought he was so wise and could get away with committing these atrocities. Margo gave Sara a quick glance and saw that Sara nodded in agreement. It was indeed time to rein in Jack and allow Margo to get on with her life.

Unbeknownst to any of them, Joe's insurance

firm capital accounts department had hired a private detective to search into Jack's past insurance policies awards. The insurance companies had begun to notice a distinct pattern of multiple marriages and claims.

Detective Johnson had been following Jack even closer now that Jack's wife, Judy, drowned off the coral reef while the foursome was snorkeling. When the detective saw them all together in one place, he came in to carry out his plan, and arrested Jack for insurance fraud, and arrested Joe under suspicion of being an accessory.

Suddenly, Joe pushed Claire out of the way, nearly knocking her over, and took off running. Jack then broke away and was right after Joe. Joe saw the police coming and darted out into the street and was struck by a delivery truck and was instantly killed. Jack took off running toward the open beach. He ran with all his might near the water's edge where the sand was most solid. Detective Johnson followed but could never catch up as he was overweight and out of shape.

Sara, and Margo seeing this, grabbed Claire's hand, beamed themselves up, and took off in Sara's silver saucer and headed for the water's edge. In a second, she was hovering over a very out of breath and frightened Jack. He appeared to be screaming as he zigzagged, running and nearly tripping several times while watching Sara's silver saucer hover over his head. She could see that he was frightened to death of the saucer. So when the three of them decided Jack had been frightened enough, they decided to use quantum energy and freeze Jack in place until Detective Johnson could catch up with Jack and handcuffed him.

Jack's run of crimes of murder, attempted murder and fraudulent insurance claims had come to an end. Jack was handcuffed and walked out feeling dumbfounded, because of his shady past life insurance claims. He was arrested and ended up in prison with a very lengthy sentence. His shady past shenanigans were made aware to everyone. Jack would be in jail for a very long time on attempted murder and three counts of murder: His first two wives, and the waitress he murdered in order to provide a body for the funeral and insurance policy collection, when he could not find Margo's in the crashed car. Judy's drowning possibly by his hands was also added to the list of deaths to be investigated.

Chapter Forty-Two

After the dreadful events were over and the detective and the police carted off Jack in handcuffs, Margo, Claire and Sara sat and talked at length. It was a terribly shocking and revealing day for Claire. First, the shock of seeing her best friend Margo who she thought was dead and buried. And then watching her husband, Joe, get stuck down dead by a delivery truck when he darted into the busy street. It was almost too much for her after earlier in the day nearly fainting at the sight of Margo. Claire cried for Joe. She had thought she had met a nice man in Joe, she had hopes for their future. But now she wondered if she might have been a future victim if Joe was becoming more like his cousin Jack. The detective had wondered why Joe did not report Jack at least to the insurance company and this made her wonder about Joe's intentions regarding her.

The three ladies sat on the restaurant patio, each trying to digest what just took place. Claire wanted to hear everything about Margo's accident. It took a while for Margo to explain everything to Claire who still seemed to be in shock by all the recent events and revelations. The bottle of wine Margo ordered seemed to help. When Margo saw that Claire was more relaxed, she explained how she met and got to know Sara.

Knowing Claire and how she may react, Margo ordered a second bottle of wine and when glasses were refilled, she began to explain to Claire how she met Sara, and how Sara came to her rescue. But she most wanted to prepare Claire for the shock that Sara was an alien, a Pleiadian from Alcyone, the Central and brightest star of the Pleiades star system.

"I knew that there was something special about you," Claire told Sara. Claire was so glad that she had the wine to help her accept this new lesson of reality of star beings coming to Earth to help us.

"I think you are pretty special yourself," Sara returned the compliment.

"Oh, you do," Claire replied, feeling very flattered. She thought Sara was gorgeous.

"When is your birthday, Claire?" asked Sara. She had a feeling Claire may be from the Pleiades too, and would be if the sun, moon, any planet, or north or south node was in the astrological birth chart in the sign of Taurus.

"My birthday is April 30th," answered Claire with a curious look.

"That means your sun sign is Taurus. I thought you were one of us," Sara stole a look at Margo.

"Welcome," Margo smiled knowing Claire was in for

a whole new adventure in learning about herself where she came from.

Sara began to explain to Claire as Margo listened on, that hybrid star beings from the Pleiades were born onto Earth to aid in human being's advancement into the Fifth Dimension of Aquarius where love and feminine energy would rise and clear the wrong doings of greedy self-serving Reptilian Anunnaki Aryan males, who had set out to establish the Illuminati a New World Order, a dictatorship. They planned a government takeover. Virus-sickened and poverty-stricken, locked in the evil clutches of a ruthless corporate backed conservative Mussolini want-to-be.

But the government overthrow efforts were halted by the liberals who were on to his emperor ways. America, as if suddenly intuitive witnessed the dawning of the Age of Aquarius and Pleiadian feminine rule. It was time for change as voters seemed tired of old white males running the show, so the country has seen more and more women go into local, state and federal politics and winning. Women challenged mostly incumbent white male politicians and won, sometimes by overwhelming numbers. It's the dawning of the Pleiadian feminine rule of the Fifth Dimension that Sara explained.

Women were forced to rise up and get into politics as conservative old white men were threatening to take away any social gains that people had made through the years. They threatened to reverse a popular president's affordable healthcare, take away women's healthcare, birth control, and abortion rights. They also wanted to end same-sex marriage rights. Women and minorities especially were tired of the old ruling conservative standards that seemed to be most negative, to the point of being cruel. It was time for the Pleiadians and the Galactic Federation to take action to reserve Earth from their own greedy, authoritarian, egotistical conservative ways that seemed to give all the breaks to the rich and either ignore or take away from the less fortunate. It was time for women to rise up and get into every level of politics they could, and so more and more women were running for political positions and winning.

Chapter Forty-Three

Margo and Claire enjoyed working together again. They worked so well together that they opened their own real estate agency. In their spare time, Margo and Claire sponsored women in politics organizations and held rallies and seminars to give women information and encourage them to run for school boards, local and state political positions. And the women rose up. Most state governments, women and minorities were now getting involved. In Washington women and minorities created a colorful and most welcomed House of Representatives, while the conservative side was still filled with all white men, but even on the conservative side more women were beginning to rise up and demand health care for all and to preserve women, minorities, and gay and lesbian rights. The two parties were beginning to work better across the aisle in order to help raise living standards across the board for all citizens.

Chapter Forty-Four

Three years had passed. Jack remained in prison. Margo and Claire were busy with their successful real estate business and sponsored political seminars. Their lives were so busy that Margo barely had much time to think about anything else but work. Until one day when Margo decided she needed a break. She went up to the cabin for a weekend visit. When she got there and all settled, she decided to take a walk to her favorite site. It was the place where she always sat on a large rock and knew that Sara was just a thought away.

It was a beautiful warm sunny day as Margo sat on the huge limestone rock. She knew that Sara was just a thought away. She meditated for a bit and then put her thoughts to Sara. In a few minutes Sara was there. Just as in the past she suddenly magically appeared. She was dressed in her usual hooded garment and floating about twelve inches off the ground.

"You summoned me, my dear," asked Sara smiling? She was happy to see Margo.

"There you are," smiled Margo, "I was missing you."

"How may I assist you, my dear?" asked Sara with a smile.

"I wanted to ask you how you thought things were going. Was life improving for those minority groups and for women in general. She asked as if she didn't know but she was well aware of the conditions on Earth had been improving but wondered if they were up to Sara's expectations. She wondered what Sara had to think about how the conditions on Earth were now. .

They talked for a while discussing how chaotic conservatives lost the presidential election and did not get a second term. Within a year and a half the liberal party had reversed and gained back all the benefits of the people that the former conservative party had taken away. People were beginning to get alone as races blended. Crime was down. Wages were increased. Healthcare benefits were revised and improved. The country was reversing the effects of global warming, more jobs were created using renewable energy. The old greedy white male buyer-beware mentality was changing as people demanded better produces and more reliable service. Patriarchal rule was gone along with the ending of the fourth Dimension and a loving Pleiadian feminine regime had emerged. There was peace on Earth. For the first time, there were no wars on Earth since the fifth dimension's arrival drove out the fourth dimensional Anunnaki Reptilians. Democracy reined. The economy was booming for everyone. There was no poverty. There was no racism, no misogyny and very low crime. Rehabilitation replaced prisons. Public schools were much improved with federal funds and free college, and there was free healthcare for everyone. The ultra-rich who had never paid any taxes for years were having to pay current and back taxes at the current rate, no more free rides or loopholes. Chief executives of corporations took less off the top and paid their workers wages that covered cost of living and more. People were paid more so they could spend more, so the economy was booming. Margo was pleased that Earth was indeed becoming as futuristic as Alcyone, we just haven't developed space capsule vehicles yet like Alcyone. But all vehicles on Earth were now electric and the air was clean and the skies deep blue again. And people were generally happy, understanding and living in harmony.

"Want to go for a ride?" asked Sara.

"Can I drive?" asked Margo.

"Of course, my dear," replied Sara.

"Where to?" asked Margo.

"Why don't we get our friend Claire and show her Alcyone, since you are both from there," suggested Sara.

"Wonderful idea," agreed Sara. They gave Claire the heads up and within minutes they were on their way to literally beam her up into Sara's silver saucer.

"Jeez, what shall I wear," clothes conscious for every occasion, Claire had wondered.

"Oh, not to worry, we have a very fine outfit for you to wear," suggested Sara.

"Oh really," responded Claire with enthusiastic expectation.

"Just throw anything on," smiled Sara, "we'll dress you when we get you here."

Margo could not wait to show Claire the one-piece matching outfit like hers that she would be wearing. And to show off to Claire her flying skills. She saw how excited Claire was and eventually handed guiding the craft over to Claire, who caught on very easily to using her thoughts to fly the craft.

The ladies enjoyed a wonderful time on Alcyone and were even more thrilled knowing they could summon Sara and visit whenever they wished and go unbeknownst by anyone. Margo loved showing her dear friend, Claire all the wonders of futuristic life on Alcyone. And if Sara's silver saucer was ever spotted and reported to the authorities. Well, the threesome knew that strict orders from on high passed down orders not to mention the sighting to the press. Still if the press did get wind of a UFO sightings, they were instructed still to not mention it to the public for fear of being fined and losing their journalists jobs. So even though government was reconstructed with more liberal politicians and the economy was booming. And there was an increase in minimum wages and equal pay for equal work for both genders; race and gender discrimination was halted by the new administration consisting of mainly women, who created laws to prevent discrimination of any kind. Equal pay for equal work bills were passed. Increases in minimum wage bills were passed.

There was better care for women's health, better schools, healthier foods and cleaner air, some things remained the same - well for the time being but promises of more positive changes were on the way. Because women are not profit margin bound and filled with egotistical greed as the men, women in charge paid more attention to saving and preserving planet Earth. With women leaders in place, the Earth rapidly rebounded and reversed the harm of deadly toxins that narcissistic egotistical leaders allowed by rolling back safeguards that had been put in place. The air, water and soil were now nearly free of all toxins. People's lives were improving. People were getting along and helping one another and gladly welcomed the feminine rule of the Fifth Dimension where love blooms and people unite for the greater good of all. Margo and Claire were most pleased with the ongoing progressive revitalization of Earth.

Chapter Forty-Five

Sara bent the rules a bit for Margo and Claire and told them that if they wished they could move from Earth and live permanently on Alcyone. That even though they were Pleiadian Hybrids born on Earth they did not have to remain on Earth if they did not want to. They would be rewarded as Margo, with the help of her best friend, Claire, had helped to enlighten spiritual beings living on Earth as human beings into the uplifting and loving energies of the Pleiadian ruled Fifth Dimension. Thus ending the Fourth Dimension of Annunaki Reptilian rule.

Planet Earth was advancing into the Fifth Dimension very nicely. Humans were advancing in technology and science. All races were blending; so there were no more racial conflicts. Finally, a truly United States, Margo and Claire agreed. It was time to hand off their duties in their political groups, sell their reality business and retire from Planet Earth and move back home to Alcyone.

Some time passed and all remained well. There was still peace on Earth. America is still a Democracy. And Margo and Claire love living on Alcyone happily experiencing new adventures. Sara helped them get acquainted with Alcyone ways and learn new ways to do things, like how to get around in those tiny capsules they have attached to their apartment balconies. When Sara felt they had gained enough confidence, Sara sent Margo and Claire out on their own in the capsule to explore Alcyone. They were always a little nervous until Sara reminded them that she was just a thought away.

But what thrilled Margo and Claire the most and even though It took Sara quite a while to teach them how to do it correctly, was hovering and gliding above the floor. Margo and Claire wern't concentrating and were drifting aimlessly about the room.

"Concentrate ladies," suggested Sara, "it's easy."

"It's not as easy as. you make it look," Claire said laughingly, as she felt that she was drifting out of control.

"It's easy, come on you can do it," egged on Sara.

"Really, it's easy," smiled Sara, "just concentrate."

"Easy, yeah you said that the first time I tried to fly your saucer too," reminded Margo.

"Learning to float above the floor is just like flying the saucer, just use your mind," suggest Sara.,

It took them a while but they finally mastered the technique of floating twelve inches above the floor just like Sara. Margo and Claire loved living on Alcyone and Sara was happy to have them home.

About the Author

This is Dianne Zimmermann's sixth novel. Her other books are *Emma's Run, Jane's Aliens, Hooch Runners, Pleasant View* and *Three Days and a Gallon of Rose* were published by BookCrafters. Dianne lives in St. Louis and enjoys writing, drawing, photography, running, hiking and road trips.